Dear Santa

KRISTEN GRANATA

Dear Santa

Kristen Granata

To everyone who struggles with their mental health during the holiday season,

We are not Grinches or Scrooges. We are the broken souls who are haunted by the memories of innocence and magic from Christmases past. Hold on to hope.

You'll find that magic again one day.

National Suicide Prevention Lifeline
1-800-273-8255

Before You Read

Dear Reader,

I wrote this novella in the matter of a week. The idea came to me in the shower (where all the best ideas come from) and I had a blast writing it. That being said, I didn't utilize an editor or Beta readers this time around. This story isn't meant to be read with a critical eye; it's not meant to hit bestseller lists; it's not meant to be taken too seriously. It's is a fast-paced, light-hearted, fun read that I wanted to give my readers for the holidays.

I hope you enjoy it!
Xo

One

Jake

"**Y**ou look familiar."

If I had a penny for every time someone said that to me, I'd have a ton of pennies to peg at people whenever they said it.

I huff out a sardonic laugh. "Yeah, I get that a lot."

The bartender twirls a strand of her blonde hair around her index finger, using her elbows to squish her tits together. "I haven't seen you here before. I'd remember you. So, where do I know you from?"

I toss back the remaining whiskey in my glass. "You don't."

She squints her blue eyes as she tries to place me.

Fuck. I really don't want to leave and find another bar right now. This dive is as empty as it's going to get in Manhattan the night before Christmas Eve, and it doesn't look like the North Pole threw up in here either.

I slide my rocks glass across the bar. "I'll take another."

She tips the bottle over my glass, filling it with amber liquid. "Are you from around here?"

"Used to be."

"What brings you back?"

"Masochism."

I enjoy torturing myself for the holidays. Drive by my parents' apartment, and pretend as if I'm going to ring the doorbell, and they'll buzz me up.

She arches a brow, and takes a step back. "Uh, okay."

Good. Stay away from me.

I've got nothing for you.

There used to be a time when I welcomed the attention from a pretty blonde. There was also a time when people knew exactly who I was. None of this *you look familiar* bullshit. But that's okay. I prefer it this way. I'd rather not have to answer their probing questions, or see the flash of judgment in their eyes. I used to be the king of this city. But that's the problem with being the king: It's a long, hard fall from your throne.

I guzzle down my whiskey, and revel in the way it dulls the ache in my chest.

The door to the bar bursts open, and a gust of frigid air whips through the small room. A woman wrapped in a ridiculous floor-length bubble jacket stomps her boots against the wooden floor. Chunks of snow trail behind her as she makes her way to an empty stool. She's wearing a bright yellow beanie, complete with a furry pompom on top, and when she pulls it off, her dark brown hair sticks up in all directions. She slides off her giant coat, revealing an oversized hot pink fuzzy sweater, and shoves her yellow mittens into her pockets before hopping into her seat.

This is what I miss about Manhattan. It's filled with quirky weirdos, and no one bats an eye.

She smiles at the bartender as she rakes her fingers through her long hair. "I'll take a glass of Pinot Noir, please."

Her eyes dart around the room as if she's looking for someone. Her gaze lingers on me for a moment, and she must decide I'm not the one she's looking for because she looks away.

The bartender fills a wine glass, and places it in front of her.

"Thank you." Dark lashes flutter against the stranger's rosy cheeks as her eyes close, and she takes three long gulps of wine.

"Rough day?" the bartender asks.

"No. Just need to calm my nerves." Her eyes skate around the bar again. "I'm meeting someone here."

The bartender smiles. "Someone special?"

Why is everyone so nosy?

She lets out an uneasy laugh. "Uh, it's sort of a blind date."

I cringe. Why would anyone go on a blind date? Do people really trust their friends *that* much? If I let my boys set me up, I'd end up sitting across the table from a man dressed as a pirate with black teeth, an eye patch and a parrot on his shoulder for two hours while they snapped pictures from the other side of the restaurant.

I've been terrified of pirates since my fourth birthday party when the impersonator showed up drunk, and trampled my presents as he fell over and vomited on my cake. *Pirates of the Caribbean* is the equivalent of a slasher movie for me.

At least, that's what my friends would've done back when we were still friends. Their check-ins have become less frequent over the years. They're moving on without me. I don't blame them. You ignore people's calls for long enough, and they'll eventually stop calling.

It's better this way.

Better for them.

After what I did, I don't deserve friends.

The bartender leans her forearms onto the top of the wooden bar. "My sister met her husband on a blind date. Maybe you'll meet your happy ending tonight too."

The brunette snort-laughs. "Is your sister's husband a male escort that her best friend convinced her to hire when she was drunk so she didn't have to deal with her mother's ridicule for another year at Christmas dinner?"

What the ...

A male escort?

The bartender's face mirrors my own bewildered expression.

"Um, no. Her husband's a dentist."

Crazy lady shakes her head. "It started as a joke, you know? My best friend, Miles, found this advice column called *Dear Santa.* People write in as if they're writing letters to Santa Claus, telling him their woes, and asking for advice. I'd had a bottle of wine that night, and I let Miles type up a letter about how I didn't want to show up to my mother's house this year alone. Again." She pauses to explain, "According to my mother, it's a cardinal sin to be single after the age of thirty."

The bartender smiles. "Moms are like that. They just want us to be happy."

I guess my mother didn't get that memo.

"Do you know what the escort looks like?"

She shakes her head. "That's part of the reason I'm so anxious. We e-mailed back and forth a few times regarding the details of our ... arrangement. He's meeting me here at seven." She tilts her wrist to check her watch. "One more hour to go."

The bartender asks the same question that's burning a hole in my brain. "Are you sure this is safe?"

She hikes a nonchalant shoulder. "The company seems reputable. They had lots of five-star ratings."

The bartender forces a tight smile, but her voice falls flat when she says, "That's good."

This is anything but *good.* An innocent young woman is meeting an escort at a dive bar down a dark alley in Manhattan. Don't get me wrong, I don't have anything against escorts. To each his own, and all. Fuck whoever you want, as long as you're not hurting anyone. But it's dangerous for a female to go off alone with a strange man. Doesn't she know this?

Either she's naïve, or she's an idiot. And New Yorkers are anything but naïve. We're look-over-your-shoulder and sleep-with-one-eye-open kind of people. She's obviously a tourist. They're crawling all over the city this time of year. Everyone comes to freeze their asses off just so they can stare up at a stupid fucking tree in the middle of a crowded street. They huddle together wearing light-up necklaces, sipping on peppermint mochas, and taking selfies in their over-the-top

Christmas sweaters that they spent money on even though they're ugly as sin, and only wear them once a year.

I watch her with narrowed lids, assessing her. She's not ugly—not on the outside, at least. Minimal makeup. Big brown eyes like a cartoon, and a cute turned-up nose on a heart-shaped face. I can't get a good look at her figure in the poncho-like sweater she's wearing, but her fingers wrapped around the wine glass look slender. Not that physical appearance matters in this situation. She could be a black belt, or a cage fighter, for all I know. Maybe she can handle herself, and that's why she isn't afraid to take a chance on meeting someone from the internet.

Still ... something tugs at my conscience.

The woman mentioned something about her mother's ridicule, and that resonates with me. I know what it feels like to be the disappointment in the family. To know that even your best isn't good enough. To be the reason for your mother's tears.

Emotion constricts my throat, and I try to swallow around it. I raise my glass, signaling for the bartender, and she heads over to me with the whiskey bottle in hand.

I down the shot, and she pours me another before returning to the peculiar woman. I lean in to listen, fully invested in this insane conversation.

"So, tell me about this agreement," the bartender says. "What happens when the escort arrives?"

"Well, I'll be taking him to my mother's cabin in Connecticut."

I choke on my spit.

She's going on a trip alone with a stranger?

"That'll give us time to get to know each other on the ride up."

Or give him time to murder you, and bury you in a ditch.

"We'll be staying there until the day after Christmas. Then, we'll come back to New York, and go our separate ways."

The bartender blows out a low whistle. "And what happens when your mom thinks you're dating this man? Won't she expect to see you two again?"

The lunatic woman pops a shoulder. "I have until Easter to figure that out."

This is the craziest thing I've ever heard.

And I've heard a *lot* of crazy shit in my time. Hell, I've been the doer of said crazy shit.

But this anxious woman fidgeting in her seat doesn't look like she's used to living on the edge. She keeps wringing her hands in her lap, and gnawing on her bottom lip. Her doe eyes shoot to the door every time it opens, followed by a breath of relief that whooshes out of her when she realizes it's not her escort.

Why is she putting herself in this situation?

Better yet, why hasn't anyone tried to stop her?

Maybe if I had someone looking out for me, I wouldn't be the washed-up has-been that I am now.

Maybe I wouldn't have to drown myself in alcohol just to keep the demons at bay.

Maybe I'd be spending Christmas with my family.

I don't know who this woman is, but I also don't know that I can sit by and watch her put herself in such a dangerous situation. And for what? To appease her mother? I chuckle to myself. If your own mother doesn't love you for who you are, then nothing you do will matter.

I scratch at the scar on my wrist as a wild idea sparks in my mind.

No, Jake.

I haven't had a home-cooked meal in ages.

You can't.

A brush of excitement tingles down my spine.

Don't do this.

My stool scrapes across the floor as I stand.

Abort!

Let's be honest, I've never really been one to listen to the voice of reason in my head.

My legs carry me over to the brunette sitting several stools away. "Hi."

She blinks up at me, and her lips part when we lock eyes.

Shit.

What if she recognizes me? This was a dumb fucking idea. I didn't think this through.

"H-hi." She swallows. "Are you ... are you him?"

Am I the former rock star who threw his entire career down the drain? Yup. That'd be me.

I open my mouth to speak, but she beats me to it. "Sorry. Of course, you're him." She sticks out her hand. "I'm Christina. Duh. You know that. It's nice to officially meet you, Dominick."

No fucking way.

She doesn't know who I am.

I clasp her hand, and give it a firm shake. "Pleasure to meet you, Christina."

She eyes the whiskey in my hand. "You've been drinking."

I gesture to her empty wine glass. "So have you."

"Just a glass to calm my nerves."

"Same here."

Her head jerks back. "I didn't think people like you got nervous. Isn't this your job?"

I cross my arms over his chest. "Just because it's my job doesn't make it any less nerve-wracking."

Her shoulders slump. "You're right. That was a rude assumption to make. I'm sorry. I guess I was so focused on my own nerves, that I didn't think you'd be nervous too. Here I was, worrying about you looking like a short, round, middle-aged man with a greasy combover, and you were probably wondering the same thing about me." A maniacal laugh rips from her throat as she keeps rambling. "This is the first time I've done something like this, you know? I'm sure you hear that all the time, but it's true. I don't really know what to expect, or how these things go. Oh, shitters. I almost forgot." She reaches for her purse, and digs around inside it. "Do I pay you up front?"

My hand flies out, and wraps around her tiny wrist. "Jesus, not now."

Her face flames. "Oh, of course. I'm sorry."

"You apologize too much."

"Sorr—" She cringes. "W-would you like to sit? Or should we get

7

going?"

Already?

I clench my jaw. "You're just going to hop into a car with a strange man?"

"Well, that's what we discussed, isn't it?"

I scrub my hand over my jaw. "And you think that's a safe decision?"

She glances at the bartender, who's been swiping a rag over the same spot on the bar several feet away. "I can drive since you've clearly been drinking. I don't mind."

"That's not what I mean." I pinch the bridge of my nose. "What if I was a rapist, or a murderer? Are you really that naïve to trust a man you found on the internet?"

Her eyes widen. "Are you saying I shouldn't trust you?"

My voice grows louder. "That's exactly what I'm saying. You shouldn't trust me, or anyone else from that stupid fucking website. You could get hurt, or worse. What's wrong with you? Why would you agree to do something like this?"

She drops her gaze to her hands in her lap, looking like a child scolded by her father.

Maybe that was a little harsh, but someone needed to tell her.

Tears well behind her lids, and she blinks them away. "I just wanted things to be normal this Christmas."

Fuck.

Guilt tugs at my heart.

I understand that feeling more than she'll ever know. She's hurting, and she doesn't want to face it alone for the holidays.

And maybe I don't either.

I collapse down onto the stool beside her. "And you thought hiring an escort would be *normal?*"

She peeks up at me from under her long lashes. "It sounds worse when you say it out loud."

One corner of my mouth tilts, and it feels strange. Can't remember the last time I smiled.

Can't remember the last time I had anything to smile about.

She tucks a strand of hair behind her ear. "Look, if you want to forget this whole thing, I get it. I'll pay you for your trouble, and you can go enjoy the rest of your night."

There's my out. I should tell her that I'm not the man she's been waiting for. She's a grown woman, and she can make her own choices—even if they are reckless and stupid. I'm not an escort, and I have no business getting involved in this situation.

But that'd mean she'd continue waiting for the *real* Dominick, and for some reason, I can't let that happen.

I heave a sigh. "We could call this off ... or we could get on the road, and get to know each other on the way to your mother's house."

A sweet smile blooms on Christina's face, and my chest cracks open.

Something raw, and wild, and real seeps out into my bloodstream.

"Let's go."

Two

Christina

Jesus, Mary, and Joseph.

Dominick is not *at all* what I expected.

Then again, I'm not well-versed on what male escorts actually look like.

I don't know why, but I pictured a man in a suit with a bowtie, like James Bond, or one of the metrosexual men that work on Wall Street—expensive-looking, with gelled hair and a fancy watch. I'm not into those types of guys anymore, so I'm almost relieved. But there's something about this man that doesn't quite put me at ease.

Dark scruff peppers his strong jawline, giving him a rugged edge. His hair falls in dark, unruly waves, and I get the urge to brush the strands out of his eyes because they're a brilliant, intense green. He has a careless air about him, in a crumpled black T-shirt and torn jeans, though his body is anything but careless. A *lot* of time and effort went into the sculpting of this body. His biceps strain through the sleeves of his shirt, the fabric taut over his broad chest and shoulders. A tease of a tattoo pokes out of his neckline, while more ink sprawls across his muscular forearm in the shape of a tribal guitar.

I specifically checked off *no tattoos* on the online form I filled out. Mom hates tattoos, and the whole point of this ridiculous plan is to make Christmas go as smooth as possible. I'd frown if I wasn't so busy drooling. This man looks dangerous. Gruff. Mysterious. The total opposite of what I'm expected to bring home.

But *my God* is he gorgeous.

After we pay our tabs, we trudge through the snow to my car.

Dominick side-eyes my hat. "You like bright colors, huh?"

"I do." I pause when we reach my lime green VW Beetle. "See?"

He grimaces, and rubs the back of his neck. "Yeah, we're not taking this to Connecticut."

"What? Why?"

"We'll take my SUV. It'll be safer in the snow."

I lift my chin. "Betsy is safe."

He lifts a brow. "Betsy?"

"My car. Betsy the Beetle."

He rolls his lips together. "Mine has four-wheel drive." He points to the blacked-out Escalade. "You can name her on the way to my apartment."

My stomach clenches. "Y-your apartment?"

Did he not read the agreement we drafted? I clearly stated that there would be no sexy time on this trip!

"I'll be quick. I just have to grab a few things. I, uh, forgot my suitcase."

A wave of relief washes over me. "Oh, of course."

I hoist my hot pink duffle out of my trunk, and sling it over my shoulder.

Dominick's head dips down. "Are those ..."

"Tiny green elephants? Yep. I found this on Canal Street. They were practically giving it away for free. How could I say no?"

He shakes his head. "You're a trip."

"Do you mind grabbing the gifts in the back?"

Snow crunches under our boots as we head to the Escalade. Dominick digs into his pocket, and pulls out his key fob. "This is a lot bigger than what you're used to driving. You think you can manage?"

"Pfft. I'll be fine. Size doesn't bother me."

A husky chuckle rumbles in his chest. "Good to know."

I slap my mitten-clad hand over my mouth, and my eyes turn to saucers. "That's not what I meant."

"Sure, it isn't."

I snatch the key out of his hand, and climb into the driver's seat, fighting the urge to bang my head against the steering wheel.

Maybe if I'm concussed, I'll miss out on Christmas altogether.

I adjust my seat, pulling it as far forward as it will go. Dominick slides in on the passenger side, stretching out his long legs in front of him. His knees would be in his chest if we took my car. This SUV will make for a much more comfortable ride.

"You wouldn't have fit anyway."

He arches a devious eyebrow at me.

"I meant in my car. Because it's so small. Gah. That's it. I'm not talking for the rest of the tip. Trip! I said trip!"

He throws his head back, and laughs. "This is going to be fun."

I grumble as I start the engine, and back out of the parking spot.

I always say the wrong things when I'm flustered, and talking to my very hot male escort is as flustered as I'll ever be.

Dominick's apartment is just over the bridge in Brooklyn. He doesn't invite me up, leaving me to my own devices in his Escalade. I search his glovebox and center console for anything incriminating or dangerous, but all I find is a handful of napkins from Starbucks, and a couple of pens.

What does his apartment look like?

Does he have a sex room, like Christian Grey?

Does he have the bodies of his former clients buried in his wall?

Heads in his freezer?

The door opens, and I jump, clutching my chest.

He arches that damn brow again. "You okay?"

I smooth my hands over the leather steering wheel. "Oh, fine. Just

13

wondering if you're a serial killer."

"Too late now." He tosses his black duffle into the back seat, and swings the door shut. "I gave you a chance to back out at the bar."

I point my index finger at him. "Just don't chop my head off when you kill me. My mother would want an open casket to say goodbye."

"I can work with that." He tilts his seat, and relaxes back against it. "So, this mother of yours. She's the reason I'm here. Tell me about her."

I blow out an exhale through my lips as I pull away from the curb. "Let's see, my father left us when I was three, and Mom had to raise us on her own. I'm the youngest of four, so she had her hands full. I don't know how she did it, honestly. I think that's why she's so hard on us. She doesn't want us to struggle the way she did."

I'm giving her a lot of credit right now. But isn't that what we do with strangers? We tell them a better version of the truth so they'll think we're just like everyone else.

"Hard on you how?"

"She isn't mean per say. Maybe rigid is a better word. She's very religious, so that doesn't help. She has strong convictions about what should and shouldn't be, and how one should and shouldn't act. She doesn't approve of my lifestyle, or my friends. I'm single, and I live in an apartment in Manhattan with my gay best friend." I chew my bottom lip. "She's not a bad person. She just ..."

"She doesn't get you," he finishes.

I glance at Dominick, and nod. "Yeah."

How can he understand that?

Then again, he's an escort. His family probably doesn't approve of his lifestyle either.

"She's the reason I took the editing job in Manhattan. I'd rather be an ant in the big city instead of under my mother's magnifying glass. My older sisters still live in Connecticut. I'm the only one who flew the coop, and Mom never lets me forget it." I straighten my shoulders. "But I had to leave. I was suffocating there."

He lets out a heavy sigh. "I get that."

We remain in silence for several minutes, lost in our own heads to the hum of the heat pushing through the vents.

"Well, that brings me to my next question." His long fingers drum on his thigh. "Why hire an escort to pretend to be your boyfriend? Why not ask someone you know, or use a dating app?"

Embarrassment tinges my cheeks, and I'm thankful for the darkness engulfing us inside the Escalade. "It was a drunken mistake." I cut him a look. "No offense."

He holds up his palms. "None taken. I've made plenty of those."

"This is the fifth year in a row that I've been single. I'm thirty-four with no husband, and no children—and I'm okay with that. I love my job, and I love my friends. But to my mother, I'm like the antichrist." I shake my head. "I just couldn't take another dinner sitting across from the disappointed look on her face. Not after how happy she was five years ago."

"What happened five years ago?"

"I was engaged to a successful lawyer, Nicholas. He checked all of my mother's boxes. He was perfect on paper. Until I caught him cheating on me with his secretary." I huff out a humorless laugh. "So cliché, I know. While I was busy planning our wedding, he was getting his eggplant sucked off under his desk at the office."

Dominick's fingertips dig into his leg. "What an asshole."

My stomach lurches at the memory, but I shrug it off. "At least I found out before the wedding. I obviously couldn't fulfill his needs."

He shoots up from his seat. "He cheated on you, and you think it's *your* fault?"

"Isn't it? People stray when they're missing something from their relationship."

The words straight from my mother's mouth.

"No. People stray because they're missing something inside themselves. You can't make someone cheat. That's on him."

I'd like to believe that, but, "I couldn't make him happy. I tried, I really did. I dressed the way he wanted me to dress. I wore my hair the way he wanted me to wear it. I stayed quiet at his work parties, because I'd always end up saying the wrong thing and embarrassing him."

"That's bullshit. You shouldn't have to change who you are for someone to love you. You're better off without that prick. Fuck him."

A surge of pride swells in my chest. "Yeah. *Fuck* him."

"Atta girl." He rolls his window down. "Come on. Say it louder. It'll make you feel better."

I press my finger to the button, and snowflakes whip against my face. "Fuck him."

"Louder, Christina." He sticks his head out the window, and roars, "Fuck him!"

I grip the steering wheel, and scream, "Fuck! Him!"

A horn blares from the car in the lane beside me, and the passenger flips me off before speeding around me.

Laughter bursts from my throat, and I scramble to roll my window back up. When I glance at Dominick, his green eyes are on me. Dimples sink into each cheek with his wide smile, and it takes my breath away.

He's beautiful when he smiles.

Dominick drops his gaze to his lap. "Thanks."

My mouth goes dry. "Did I say that out loud?"

"Yeah, you did."

"Shitters."

"I like that I don't have to guess what's on your mind." He picks at the frayed threads on his jeans. "Most people keep their thoughts to themselves, and you're left wondering what they're really thinking about you."

Nick hated that about me. Funny how one person can like the very thing another person hated about you.

The snow comes down harder, and I ease up on the gas. "Does your family know what you do for a living?"

He turns to look out the window. "No."

Ah, sore subject.

"Are you close with them?"

"No."

"Do you have any siblings?"

"No."

16

Okay, I need to stop asking yes or no questions.

"How did you get into ... your line of work?"

He clears his throat. "Look, we only have a few hours to get our story straight before we get to your Mom's house. If I'm going to be your fake boyfriend, then we need to make it believable."

He's right. I shouldn't be trying to get to know the escort I hired—I need to get to know my new boyfriend.

"Sorry. I didn't mean to pry into your personal life."

He swings his gaze back to me. "You don't have to be sorry. I just don't want to mess this up for you. We need to come up with answers to the questions your family will ask about our relationship."

"All right. The first things anyone will ask is how we met, and what your profession is." I rub my forehead. "How we met is easy. Lots of options in Manhattan. But I've been stumped on what to say you do that won't insight too many hard-to-answer follow-up questions."

He ponders a moment. "What if we say we met at work? You know a lot about what you do, so you can field those questions for me if I get stuck. Won't be too hard to believe either." He gestures to his outfit. "I don't exactly look like a stock broker."

"Hmm. That's actually a great idea."

Mom doesn't disapprove of my career, and I wouldn't have to chance making a slip-up in front of my family. Lying to them about my relationship will be difficult enough. The simpler our story is, the better.

Dominick eases back against the seat, and listens while I tell him about my job for the next thirty minutes.

My phone dings with a series of texts, and I jerk my thumb over my shoulder. "Do you mind grabbing my phone? It's in the inside pocket of my purse."

Dominick unclips his seatbelt, and twists around in his seat to rummage through my bag. "Do you really need all this stuff in here? You look like you're ready for the apocalypse."

I snort. "Christmas dinner with my family makes *The Walking Dead* look like *Sesame Street*."

"That's comforting." He switches on the dome light above us. "Got it." He plops back into his seat holding a small silver tube. "And you needed *this* for Christmas dinner?"

My eyes pop, and heat spreads up my neck and into my cheeks like a flashfire. "That ... that's just lipstick."

The jerk pulls off the cap, and flicks the switch on the bottom. A loud buzzing fills the SUV. "Oh, I think this is for a different set of lips."

I reach for the mini-vibrator, and the steering wheel veers to the right. "Damnit. Put that away. You're going to make me crash."

Laughing, he turns it off, and squints as he holds it up in front of his face. "This is awfully small. Do you insert it, or ...?"

"Oh, my God. We are *not* having this conversation."

"Why not?" He pokes my arm with my vibrator. "Shouldn't you be able to talk to your *boyfriend* about this sort of thing?"

I reach for it again, but he swats my hand away.

I growl. "Until we arrive at my mother's house, you are not my boyfriend."

He chuckles, and tosses it back into my purse. "Okay, okay. Here's your phone."

I unlock it, and hand it back to him. "Can you read the texts to me? I don't want to take my eyes off the road."

"Your mom says: The snow is really coming down here. You should make the trip in the morning. Don't drive in this."

I chew my bottom lip as I stare out at the blustery snow hitting the windshield. We're already on our way. I don't want to turn back now. Plus, I might come to my senses in the morning, and I'd lose my $500 deposit on Dominick.

Yes, I put a down-payment on my date. Family makes you do crazy things.

"You also have a few texts from Miles. He wants to know if your escort is hot." Dominick's thumbs tap across the screen.

"Hey, what are you writing? Don't text him back."

"Already hit *Send*." He chuckles to himself. "Think about it though: How are we supposed to convince your family we're together

18

if we don't act like a couple? We should be able to discuss uncomfortable things with each other, and more than just your trusty vibrator."

He has a point.

My anxiety level rises. "I didn't think this through. We can't fabricate an entire relationship during one car ride. My mother will sniff out our lie like a bloodhound. She's relentless. This was such a bad idea. What was I thinking? I can't do this. I'm a terrible liar. Why did I think I could do this?"

Dominick's large hand comes down on my shoulder. "Relax, Rainbow Brite. Everything's going to be okay. I have a plan."

Three

Jake

I've officially gone off the deep end.

I thought I was mental before, but this really takes the cake.

What the hell am I doing?

I'm lying to this poor woman—pretending to be an escort, of all things. My conscience is screaming at me to tell her the truth. Come clean now, before we go any further.

But the fucked up side of my brain reminds me that I'm doing Christina a favor. She's better off with me than the real Dominick. A hell of a lot safer, too. And if I can't save face with my own family, then maybe I can help her with hers.

"One queen bed, or two twins?"

"The queen is fine."

Christina's spine stiffens. "Uh, Dominick ... can I speak with you for a sec?"

"Excuse us, Madeline."

Madeline smiles. "Of course."

Christina digs her little claws into my forearm, tugging me away from the counter. "Why did you choose a queen bed?"

I shrug. "It'll be more comfortable. I'm too big for a twin."

She glares at me. "And what about me? I'm not comfortable sleeping in the same bed. I don't know what you're expecting here, but we agreed—"

I hold up my hand. "I'm not expecting anything except for a good night's sleep. The snow is getting worse. Even your mother told you to find a place to stay for the night. Plus, where do you think we'll be sleeping at your mother's cabin? Won't it look strange if we sleep in separate rooms?"

Her shoulders drop. "I didn't think of that."

I tip her chin to bring her worried eyes back to mine. They're wide, blinking up at me from under the yellow hat. "I promise you, I will not touch you. We're just sleeping."

She pulls her bottom lip between her teeth, drawing my full attention. Those lips are dangerous. Full and pouty, the bottom plumper than the top, I fight the urge to lean in and bite it.

After discovering the little toy she carries in her purse, my mind has been in the gutter. But I need to rein it in. Christina is nothing like the women I've been with in the past. Band groupies with heavy makeup and revealing outfits. Wild party girls looking for a good time. They flaunted what they had, and spread their legs for the money or the fame—or both. It was fun in the beginning, but it got old fast. And once I made headlines for reasons other than my band, women stopped throwing themselves at me.

What would Christina think of me if she knew who I really was?

Same as everyone else, I assume.

When we get our room key, we take our bags up to the second floor. Christina mutters to herself on the elevator ride. I've only spent an hour with her, yet I've quickly learned that she talks to herself when she's nervous. It's fun to watch. This woman is definitely entertaining.

Just as we reach our room, a young couple stops in the middle of the hallway.

"Oh, shit," the man says. "Are you Jake Fallon?"

My stomach bottoms out. "Nah, man. Sorry." I angle myself away

22

from them, and fumble with the key card.

"Are you sure? Because you look just like Jake Fallon."

I clench my teeth as I jiggle the door handle. "I'm sure."

Why do hotel keys never work?

"That dude was incredible," he continues to the woman on his arm. "One of the best guitar players to ever live. Shame what happened to him."

Christina peers out from behind me. "What happened to him?"

The light on the door turns green, and I blow out a breath of relief. "Come on, get in." I usher her into the room before the man can answer her question, and slam the door closed behind us.

Christina's eyebrows dip. "Geez, you don't have to push me."

"Sorry." I scratch the back of my neck. "I think that guy was drunk. Didn't want him to start any trouble."

"You're a little paranoid. Anybody ever tell you that?" She flips on the lights, tosses her jacket onto a chair, and walks in a circle around the room—giving me the perfect view of her thick ass and thighs in her tight jeans.

Damn. Wasn't expecting that underneath the bulky coat. Makes me wonder what else she's hiding under the big fuzzy sweater ...

Head out of the gutter, Jake.

"This place is nice." She drops down onto the corner of the bed, and bounces, putting more filthy images in my mind. "I'm not tired." She glances at her watch. "It's too early to go to sleep. Let's look up that Jake Fallon guy, and see if you really look like him."

"No." It comes out too quick and harsh, so I backtrack. "We need this extra time to prepare for tomorrow."

She huffs out a sigh. "You're right. I'm just so nervous about this. I hate lying, especially to my family."

I lower myself onto the mattress beside her. "Some lies are okay, as long as they don't hurt people. You're not lying to hurt your mother. You're trying to protect yourself. There are worse things in the grand scheme of life."

She glances at me from the corner of her eye. "Easy for you to say. You lie for a living."

I know she's talking about being an escort, but the same rings true for my life in the limelight. So many nights, I had to put on a show when all I wanted to do was break down and cry. Being on stage with thousands of fans screaming my name became a prison sentence. I was locked into my contract with the record label, and I was forced to portray this charismatic rock god, night after night, in city after city. I pretended to be okay. I acted like I could handle it. I lied to my band, I lied to my family, and I lied to myself. Instead of admitting the truth, I spiraled so far down into the depths of my lie that it almost killed me.

Christina's soft hand covers mine, and I didn't realize I'd been rubbing my scar, lost in thought. "Hey, are you okay? I'm sorry I said that. I didn't mean it as rude as it came out."

"I told you to stop apologizing for the things you say. I like it when you tell me what's on your mind."

Her cheeks blush a pretty pink, and her hand jerks back as if touching me burns her skin.

"It's okay to touch me, you know." I thread my fingers through hers. "Girlfriends touch their boyfriends all the time."

Her face tinges a shade darker than before, and I want to follow the flush along her neck to see how far down it goes.

"I guess we should talk about how we're going to act in front of my family." She stares down at our hands. "My ex wasn't big on PDA."

"Fuck him, remember?" I shift to face her. "Tell me what you're comfortable with, what you like—not what anyone else told you that you should like."

She holds up our interlaced hands. "I like holding hands."

"Got it. What else?"

She takes her bottom lip between her teeth, and tilts her head as she gazes up at me. "I'd like it if we could touch each other's hair." She reaches out, and pushes back my hair, raking her nails over my scalp.

A flash of heat trails down my body, straight to my dick.

Down, boy.

All she did was touch my hair to get me hard. Has it really been that long?

I need to take control of this situation. I brush a strand of hair off her face, and tuck it behind her ear, letting my knuckles skate down her delicate jawline. Her skin is creamy and soft, and she smells like pineapple and coconuts.

She shivers, and pops up from bed, putting distance between us. "That's good. Tender and sweet. It's perfect."

I remain on the bed, and adjust the seat of my pants.

Focus, man. "So, how long have we been dating?"

Christina taps a finger against her chin. "One month. That would explain away any nervousness I have around you."

I shake my head. "One month, and you're bringing me around for the holidays?"

"How about six months then?"

I arch an eyebrow. "Six months, and you haven't told your mother about me?"

She lets out a frustrated sigh. "Let's say two months, and we were friends before that."

"That works. We got to know each other at the office, and went for drinks after. We hit it off, and then I asked you out on a date."

She crosses her arms. "Why can't I be the one who asked you out? It's the twenty-first century, you know."

I throw my hands up. "Fine. You asked me out."

She paces the room, twisting the end of her hair around her finger. "What do we call each other? Pet names are important."

I grin. "I like calling you Rainbow Brite."

"I'm not sure I like that." She frowns. "It feels like you're making fun of me."

My eyebrows lift. "I'm definitely not making fun of you. You dress in bright colors. It's ... unique."

She shoots me a disbelieving look. "Unique means weird."

"That's not what I meant. Unique means rare. Unlike the rest. You stand out in a room, and you don't flaunt your body to garner that attention. You're all covered up, which leaves more to the imagination." I lean back on my elbows, letting my eyes trail down her body. "And I have a very vivid imagination."

Her face turns the deepest red I've seen thus far, and her fingers fidget with the hem of her sweater. "Stop looking at me with sexy eyes."

I smirk. "Why? How else is a boyfriend supposed to look at his girlfriend?"

She plants her hand on her hip. "Would you like it if I looked at you like a stick of man meat?"

I bark a laugh. "That is the *only* way a man wants a woman to look at him."

She rolls her eyes. "My mother is religious. You can't be ogling my goodies over the Christmas ham."

I push off the bed, and stretch my arms over my head. "Don't worry, Rainbow Brite. No one will see me ogling your goodies." Her eyes drop to the sliver of skin peeking out as my shirt rides up my stomach. "But maybe you'll be the one having trouble keeping your eyes off *my* goodies."

"It was an involuntary reaction. You stretched, and your shirt went up, and my eyes went there." She waves a hand. "Totally innocent."

I chuckle. "Whatever you say."

"You're in shape. You must work out a lot."

I hike a shoulder. "It helps take the edge off."

"Must be good for business. I'm sure you have a lot of satisfied customers." She leans against the dresser. "How long have you been doing this?"

I scrub a hand over my jaw. "I'd rather not discuss this. Let's stick to the story."

She lets out a grunt of disappointment. "What about your family? My mom might ask about your parents."

"My mother's a teacher, and my father's a postal worker."

"You mentioned you're not close with them. Is it because of your job?"

I blow out a sigh. "Yes. But I'll have to embellish that story for your mother."

"Let's tell her they live far away. This way, it explains why you didn't go home for the holidays since you're spending it with me."

I nod. "Smart."

She runs her fingers through her hair as she paces. "What else are we leaving out? I know we're going to forget something."

She looks so stressed, I cross the room and cup her shoulders. "Whatever your family throws at us, we'll handle. One of us will say something, and the other will go along with it."

Her big brown eyes look up at me, hope and trust emanating from her warm gaze.

I don't deserve it.

She reaches up, and caresses my face with both hands. The gentle touch almost brings me to my knees. "You're not what I expected."

That makes two of us.

On the outside, she's eccentric with her bright colors, and nervous rambling. But there's something about her that calls out to me—something broken and fragile, like a wounded bird who longs to fly and be free. Mom always used to say, "We see ourselves reflected in others." I never really understood it before.

Being with Christina, I'm starting to get the meaning.

"Thank you for doing this for me," she says. "I know it's your job, but ... I feel better knowing I have someone on my side."

"We're a team. I've got your back, Rainbow Brite."

A soft smile touches her lips.

"Why don't you take advantage of the big bathtub we have for the night? Unwind, and try to relax."

She nods, and turns toward the bathroom.

I collapse back onto the bed, and flip on the TV to distract myself from thoughts of Christina taking off her clothes on the other side of the wall. There's a Christmas movie playing on every station, and I can't help but chuckle to myself when I land on *Love, Actually.* My best friend, Trent, loves this movie. He swore me to secrecy after he made me watch it one year, and he bawled like a baby. To this day, I've honored that oath.

I cried, too. It's a good fucking movie.

Sorrow burns deep in my chest like a hot branding iron. I haven't talked to Trent in months. He says he's not mad at me, but how could he not be? He was my partner in crime. We toured the country together. Close as brothers. And yet I couldn't ask him for help when I needed it. Maybe it was pride. Maybe I was too embarrassed to let him see that side of me. Or maybe I just didn't want to burden him with my problems.

I slip my phone out of my back pocket, and open Instagram. I never post anything, but every now and then, I like to see how everyone's doing.

Without me.

Like I said, I'm a masochist.

Trent and his wife had their second baby last month. His family's smiling faces fill my screen. As happy as I am for him—and I am beyond happy for him, because he deserves the world—I can't help but wonder why that life couldn't have been in the cards for me too.

Didn't I deserve to be happy?

I lose myself in the downward spiral until I hear the glug of the drain in the bathtub, rocketing me back to reality.

The bathroom door flies open, and I'm about to ask Christina how her bath was, but her screeching voice stops me in my tracks.

"You have a lot of explaining to do, Jake Fallon!"

Oh, shit.

Four

Christina

I stomp out of the bathroom, clutching the towel that's wrapped around my body.

Dominick—or Jake—whoever the hell this man is, sits up on the bed with wide eyes.

I shove my phone in his face. "No wonder that guy in the hallway thought you looked like Jake Fallon. Because you freaking *are* Jake Fallon!"

All I wanted was a nice, relaxing bubble bath. I'd texted Miles to fill him in on my whereabouts, and he asked what my escort looked like. After describing him in great detail, I thought, *hmm, I should look up this Jake Fallon dude and see if he resembles Dominick.*

I almost died from shock and drowned in a hotel bathtub.

Dominick doesn't *resemble* the former lead guitarist of some rock band I've never heard of. Oh, no. He either has an identical twin, or he *is* him.

This doesn't make any sense. Why would someone who's rich and famous work as an escort?

Dominick/Jake rises from the bed with both palms facing me. He approaches me like he's creeping toward a scared animal. I must look like a feral cat. My chest heaves, my damp hair sits in a knotted bun on top of my head, and there's water dripping down my skin. But I don't care what I look like right now. I need answers. I need to know why my escort looks like a famous rock star.

"I can explain." His voice is low and calm, but his expression reads, *Oh, shit. I'm caught.*

I back away with each step he takes. "You can start by telling me your real name."

His hands fall to his sides. "Can you please stop inching away from me? I'm not going to hurt you."

"And how do I know that? Hmm?" I fling my arms out wide, but my towel unravels, and I'm quick to catch it before it opens. "You said your name was Dominick, and now I find out you're exactly who that guy in the hallway thought you were. You lied to me. What the hell is going on?"

"Please, calm down. I will give you the truth. Just sit, and listen."

He looks so worried, I almost feel sorry for him.

Almost.

I snatch a pillow from the bed, and launch it at him. "Don't tell me to calm down!"

He dodges the flying pillow. "I'm sorry."

I fling another pillow. "You should be!"

He catches this one. "I am, okay? Just stop throwing things at me so I can explain."

My eyes dart to the lamp on the nightstand.

"Christina, please. Don't hurt the lamp."

With an exasperated huff, I cross my arms, and sit on the corner of the bed. "Fine. But you need to stay over by the window in case I need to push you out of it."

His lips twitch.

I close one eye, and point a finger at him. "Do not test me."

He makes a cross over his heart, and leans against the windowsill.

"My name is Jake Fallon, and I'm not really an escort."

Heat rushes into my cheeks as fear licks up my spine. "Oh, my God. Are you a murderer? Are you going to chop my body up into tiny pieces, and eat me for dinner?" I clamp my hand over my mouth. "I think I'm going to be sick."

"No!" He grimaces, and roughs a hand through his hair. "I'm not a murderer. I swear, Christina. I won't hurt a single hair on your head."

"Then why are you pretending to be someone else?"

"I overheard you telling the bartender about driving off with an escort, and I … I was worried. You seemed like an innocent naïve woman, and I didn't want anything to happen to you." He glances down at the hunter green carpet. "I heard what you said about your mother, and I know what it feels like to be alone on Christmas. I felt bad."

My stomach clenches. "So, why not just tell me that from the start? Why go along with this charade?"

He heaves a sigh, and leans his head back against the window. "Would you have gotten in the car with me if you thought I was someone other than your escort?"

I chew my bottom lip. "Probably not."

He hikes his shoulders. "I couldn't let you walk out of the bar with some strange man. I knew with me, at least you'd be safe."

I bark out a laugh. "Safe with a lying jerk?"

He frowns. "I'm sorry, Christina."

"Stop saying my name all husky and sexy like that. You don't get to be sorry. You lied." My head tilts. "Tell me, Jake Fallon: What are you getting out of this? You're a celebrity, apparently. You don't need the money."

His expression changes, and absolute sincerity reflects in his eyes. "I-I didn't want to spend another holiday alone. Figured we could help each other."

Silence fills the space between us.

Don't feel bad for him, Christina. This could be part of his plan. Weaken your defenses, and then attack you when you let your guard down.

"Why are you alone?" I fiddle with the edge of my towel. "Did you murder your whole family, and now you're on the run?"

He closes his eyes, and pinches the bridge of his nose. "Would you stop with the whole murderer thing? I've never killed anyone in my life. And you weren't too worried about getting murdered when you agreed to get in the car with an escort."

I hate that he has a point.

Jake pushes off the window, and slumps onto the bed beside me. "To be honest, I don't understand it either. I shouldn't have lied to you, but I saw you sitting there waiting for someone to walk into the bar, and I just couldn't let you leave not knowing if you'd be okay. It was an impulsive decision, and I'm sorry. But I never meant to hurt you, or scare you."

I suppose this would be an elaborate plan to kill me—if he was going to do it, he would've done it already.

I look away from his gaze. I'm unable to maintain my wits when I look into those beautiful, somber eyes of his. "I just don't understand. Why would you care about what happens to a woman you don't even know?"

He's quiet at that, and when I glance at him, it looks like he's struggling with some internal battle.

"Jake, I need an answer. You owe it to me."

He rests his elbows on his knees, and his head sinks into his hands. I ball my fingers into fists to keep me from smoothing them down his back. Right now, the big bad rock star doesn't seem so big. Or bad.

He looks like someone who needs a friend.

A shiver runs through me, still damp from the bath wearing nothing but a towel.

Jake peeks at me out of the corner of his eye. "Why don't you get changed, and we'll talk. I'll tell you anything you want to know."

I drag my enormous elephant bag into the bathroom, and slip into my sweats. I comb through the tangles in my hair, and let it air dry. When I emerge from the bathroom, Jake is waiting for me in a chair that faces the bed. His hair is a disheveled mop from running his fingers through it so many times, and the muscles in his forearms are coiled tight while his knee bounces.

Why is he so nervous?

I sit in the middle of the bed, and crisscross my legs. "All right. Let's hear it. And if you even think about lying to me again, I'll Google your name and find out the truth."

He blows out a stream of air through his plump lips. "You can look me up, but just remember that the media spins everything. Some of what you'll find is true, and those are the parts I'm going to tell you."

I reach for one of the pillows remaining on the bed after my temper tantrum, and hug it against my chest. "That's fair."

"I was the lead guitarist of My Two Faces. I loved it. Performing was my passion. But the lifestyle of being famous, and going on tour, wears on you." He rubs at a scar on his wrist, and the muscles in his jaw pop. "I, uh … I suffer with depression." His eyes flick to mine for a brief second before dropping back down to his lap. "I had to battle with that while being in the limelight, and it wasn't easy. I was drinking a lot, going to parties after our shows, and I spiraled. Things got out of control."

My chest aches. I wasn't prepared for this. I want to comfort him. Wrap my arms around him, and tell him that everything's going to be okay. I've never experienced depression before, but I know how serious a mental illness can be.

He clears his throat, and continues. "One night after a show in Miami, I went back to my hotel room, and …" Tears fill behind his lids, and he blinks up at the ceiling. "I tried to take my own life."

A gasp leaves my throat, and I cover my mouth with my hands.

Oh, my God.

Jake tried to kill himself?

Why on earth would he want to do something like that?

He huffs out a humorless laugh, and a lone tear slides down his cheek. "My best friend found me on the bathroom floor. He had a couple of girls with him, and they wanted to party with the two of us. I was rushed to the hospital, and the next day, I was on the cover of every tabloid in the country. I didn't even get to tell my parents what happened before they saw it on TV."

I don't know what to say to that. I can't fathom ever feeling so low that I'd want to end my life. I've been heartbroken, sure. I've felt crappy after a barrage of insults from my mother. But I've *never* wanted to *die.*

Jake brings his eyes to mine. "Say something."

My bottom lip trembles. "What does someone say to something like that?"

He pops a shoulder. "People have had plenty to say."

"Like your family?"

He nods.

And I get it.

Between her religious beliefs, and her tough attitude, my mother would disown me if I attempted to commit suicide. She wouldn't understand. She'd tell me I was weak, or being dramatic.

I scoot to the edge of the bed, and take Jake's hands in mine. "I'm so sorry you went through that, and I'm sorry you didn't have anyone to stand by your side to help you. Nobody deserves to feel that way." I swallow past the lump in my throat. "And I know we just met, but I'm glad you're alive."

Jake's head snaps up, and his eyes widen with disbelief. "Thank you for saying that."

I squeeze his hands. "I'm not just saying it, Jake. I mean it. My mother used to read from the bible when I was younger, and she'd talk about how God has a plan for us. Everything that happens, everything that gets put in our path, is predestined." I shake my head, and a soft laugh escapes me. "I'm not sure I believe everything she clings to in that book, but meeting you in that bar tonight? It doesn't seem so random. Maybe it's a coincidence, but maybe not. Maybe we can help each other through the holiday."

He tilts his head, and his eyes search my face. "I know I apologized for lying to you, but I don't regret it. I'd rather be here, with you, than back in the bar alone."

I pull my bottom lip between my teeth, physically stopping the words, *Me too,* from tumbling out of my mouth.

I know that doesn't make it any less true, but right now, it's what I need to cling to. There's a strange sense of relief washing over me that I don't comprehend. I'm glad Jake isn't an escort. It makes this whole situation less humiliating for me. And I'm happy to know I'm helping him too.

"My parents don't understand why I did what I did." Jake's thumb strokes the top of my hand, and I'm not sure he even knows he's doing it. "My dad told me it was selfish, and that I should've thought about how it would've affected him and my mother." He shakes his head. "It strained our relationship so much that I don't even know how to be around them anymore. It makes me angry to think that they're mad at me for this. It's like being angry at someone for getting cancer."

"They sound a lot like my mother. She's always making it about her."

He nods. "It's nice to have someone to talk to about this. Thank you for listening."

Sliding my hands away from his, I rake them through my damp hair. "You know, it's kind of ironic that the name of your band is My Two Faces."

His shoulders shake as he laughs. "You're not going to forgive me for lying, are you?"

I squint one eye. "Eh, I think I need to sleep on it."

The truth is, I forgave him the second after he shared his personal story with me. But I'm not ready for him to know that. I've found that when people learn you're a forgiving person, they tend to do more things that need forgiving.

"Then let's get to bed. We've got a long ride ahead of us tomorrow." Jake stills. "Unless you don't want me to come with you anymore."

"Oh, you're not getting out of this so easily, Jake Fallon. If you survive Christmas dinner with my mother, then you'll earn your redemption."

We climb under the covers, and each of us scoots to our respective edge of the bed.

I reach over, and switch off the lamp. Staring into the darkness, I listen to Jake's even breaths, trying to match it with my own, but it's no use. My skin hums from the proximity of his warm body lying next to me.

A few hours ago, I was waiting for an escort in a bar. Now, I'm sleeping next to a rock star in a hotel room.

Life's crazy.

"Jake?"

"Yeah?"

"I like Jake better than Dominick."

His gravely laughter sends a delicious shiver down my spine.

"And Jake?"

"Yes, Christina."

"If I find out that you're lying about the whole depression thing, you know I'm going to chop your balls off, right?"

"I wouldn't expect anything less."

Five

Jake

*F*uck *yes, Christina. Just like that …*

"Jake! Wake up!"

My eyes pop open, and I stifle a groan.

Just a dream, asshole.

Christina hugs her knees to her chest on the other side of the bed, eyes wide. "You were having a dream."

I roll onto my back, and throw my arm over my eyes. "A damn good one, too."

"I can tell."

Her clipped tone has me peeking out from under my arm. "Was I talking in my sleep?"

Her cheeks tinge with pink, and she gestures to the sheet covering my legs. "Your body was doing the talking."

I glance down at the tent pitched in my boxers. "What's the matter, Rainbow Brite? All men get morning wood."

She arches an eyebrow. "Do all men hump the person they're

sleeping next to?"

A loud laugh rips from my chest. "I was humping you?"

She gives me an emphatic nod. "Like an over-excited dog."

I can't help but laugh harder. "I'm sorry. I didn't know what I was doing."

"I told myself the same thing when I woke up to your rhythmic gyrating—until I heard my name."

Rhythmic gyrating? Who talks like this?

I turn onto my side, and prop my head up with my hand, shooting her a wink. "I told you it was a damn good dream."

Her pink lips part, and a blush steals up her neck.

"Relax," I say, more to myself than to her. "I'll take a cold shower, and everything will be fine."

My shower is the opposite of cold. I rub one out, finishing the end of the dream that was so rudely interrupted. Christina bent over on all fours, her hair fanned out against her bare back while I give it a good tug, and plunge into her from behind …

Damn. This girl has me worked up, and I haven't even kissed her.

Besides my therapist, I haven't opened up to anyone about what happened when I tried to kill myself. I haven't wanted to. But looking into Christina's honest brown eyes last night, I felt compelled to tell her everything. And her reaction was filled with more compassion and understanding than anyone has shown me.

With her, I feel seen. I feel accepted.

We grab breakfast on the road, and set out on the highway.

I glance at Christina in the passenger seat. She's lost in thought gazing out the window, wearing another pair of tight jeans, and a loose emerald green cardigan. She's buttoned every button, which only makes me that much more curious about what she's covering up.

"You're quiet this morning." I nudge her knee with the back of my hand. "You still mad at me?"

She shakes her head, but her eyes don't meet mine. "No. Yes, but no."

"Because that's not confusing at all."

"I get why you did what you did. You weren't lying to hurt me.

You were trying to protect me." Finally, she flicks those big beautiful eyes to mine. "Just don't lie to me again."

I bite back a smile. "I won't. I promise."

She hums her response, and returns her gaze out the window. I'd give my left nut to know what she's thinking about. She's not quiet by nature—she must be pondering something important.

Unease coils around my stomach.

"Christina, your silence is freaking me out. Are you okay? If it has to do with what I told you last night—"

"What was your dream about?"

I sputter. "What?"

"The dream you had this morning." She waves a hand, gesturing to my dick. "The one that made your salami hard."

"My *salami?*" I choke out a laugh. "You really are something else. That's what you've been thinking about all morning?"

She grimaces, and her head falls back against the headrest. "Yes! It's kind of hard not to wonder what's happening when a guy is thrusting into you in his sleep, moaning your name in your ear, okay? I'm curious—sue me!"

I'm equal parts humored and turned on.

My rainbow girl wants to hear about how I fucked her in my dream.

"Like, where were we? What were we doing? What was I wearing?" She throws her hands in the air. "I need details."

I give her a sideways glance. "Not sure where we were exactly. In a bed. The lights were dim, but I could see you perfectly. You were on your hands and knees—"

"Oh, my God. I was doing it *doggy style?*" She covers her face with her hands.

"Yeah, what's wrong with that?"

She peeks between her fingers, and whispers, "I've never done it like that before."

My SUV swerves to the right, and I grip the steering wheel to recover. "Are you shitting me? You've never had a man take you from behind?"

She shakes her head. "I'm not some sex-crazed rock star like you."

My eyebrows hit my hairline. "Excuse me? Who says I'm sex-crazed?"

"I don't know. Aren't all rock stars sluts? You have women throwing themselves at you everywhere you go."

She's not wrong, but I mess with her anyway. "I'm offended, Christina. I can't believe you'd believe a stereotype like that."

"I-I didn't mean to … I just thought … I assumed …"

I chuckle. "I'm fucking with you. Of course rock stars are sluts. It's like an all-you-can-eat buffet every night of the week."

Her adorable nose crinkles. "Gross. I hope you were careful."

I hold up three fingers. "I always wrapped it up. I love my dick too much to let it shrivel up with an STD. But we got off topic here. Let's get back to the part where you've never been fucked from behind."

Her cheeks turn my favorite color pink, and she shrugs. "My ex never asked."

"And what about you? What did you want?"

She fidgets in her seat. "I don't know."

"Of course you do. Everybody knows what they like. They're just not always comfortable enough to tell their partners."

She nods. "I wasn't myself with him."

"So, what's your kink? What's the real you into? You know, besides lipstick-shaped vibrators."

She growls. "You need to forget you ever saw that."

I grin. "Not a snowball's chance in hell, sweetheart."

She huffs out a frustrated sigh. "I'm not into anything crazy. I mean, I'd like to think I'm open to suggestions in the bedroom." She chews that sexy-as-sin bottom lip. "I'd just like to have an orgasm every once in a while. I don't think that's too much to ask for."

My wheel jerks to the right again. "What do you mean *every once in a while*?"

"With my ex, it was all about him. The next time I have sex with someone, I'd want it to be about pleasing me."

Whoa, whoa, whoa.

Hold on a fucking second. "Are you saying that the last time you had sex was with your ex-fiancé five years ago?"

She groans, and hides behind her hands again. "That sounds so much worse when you say it like that."

The thought of this beautiful woman never being with someone who made her feel like a queen blows my mind. The things she hasn't experienced … the way I could worship her body … I'm so hard, I could break through steel.

"Say something," she says, her brown eyes pleading. "I'm mortified that I told you any of this."

I shake my head, hoping to shake the thoughts of her naked body out of my mind. "Rainbow Brite, you don't know all the dirty, filthy thoughts running through my mind right now."

She giggles, as if I'm joking.

I need to change the subject before I poke a hole through my jeans. "We haven't kissed, you know. Couples kiss in front of their families."

"Not my family."

I arch a brow. "Your mother has four daughters. How do you think that came to be?"

She sticks out her tongue, and makes a gagging noise. "I don't ever want to think about how that came to be."

Feeling bold, I slide my palm over her thigh. "What about this? Is this allowed around your mother?"

She sucks in a sharp breath, and goes stiff in the seat. "Uh, sure. I guess."

"It won't work with that terrified look on your face."

She eases back against the seat, and drags her delicate fingers up and down my arm. "How's this?"

A strangled noise leaves my throat. "Yeah, that's good."

Just keep touching me, rainbow girl.

We drive another mile, giving each other gentle caresses, nothing too daring.

Then the tips of her fingers brush against the scar on my wrist, and I yank my arm out of her grasp.

She jumps. "I'm sorry. Did I hurt you?"

I clench my jaw, my lungs constricting. "I ... it's ..."

Christina takes my hand, and lays my arm back on her lap.

I let her.

She turns it over, and peers down at the raised trail of skin. "Is this ..."

I swallow, drowning in shame. "Yes."

She lifts my arm, and brings it to her lips, placing the most tender kiss to my scar.

My heart thunders in my chest.

"We all have scars, whether you can see them or not." She kisses my wrist again. "They remind us that life is short, and sometimes we make mistakes. But the important thing is that we're still here—we're still living to fight another day."

My vision blurs, and I struggle for my next breath.

"You don't have to be ashamed of this." Her voice floats over me like a soothing song. "Not around me."

What I would've given to hear someone say these words to me three years ago. Yet here she is, this near stranger, and she's accepting me, understanding me, more than anyone in my life ever has.

"You're something special, rainbow girl." I glance at her before returning my eyes to the road. "You're like the whole damn pot of gold waiting at the end of it."

Her soft flutter of laughter warms me to my core. "Can I ask you something?"

I nod. "Sure."

"Can you sing?"

My head jerks back. "Are you asking me *to* sing, or *if* I can sing?"

She shrugs. "Whichever you'll give me."

I laugh. "Yes, I can sing. Been a while since I've done it though."

She closes her eyes, and places her palm flush to her chest. "I bet you sound amazing. Your voice is—"

"Husky and sexy, as you put it."

She grins. "It is."

Normally, I'd be turned off by a woman asking about my life in the band. Groupies always asked the same trivial questions. They weren't interested in the person I was off stage. I was a monkey to wind up. A roller coaster to ride. An accomplishment to brag to their friends about.

But with Christina, it's different.

I'm noticing that *everything* is different with her.

Which is why I lean forward, and switch on the radio to search for the perfect song to serenade her with.

After a flipping past a few commercials, and a country song, I find what I'm looking for. I crank up the volume, and clear my throat.

Amusement flashes in Christina's eyes, and she twists in her seat to face me.

She doesn't think I'm going to do it.

Oh, rainbow girl. So much to discover about me.

I start low, singing along with the slow croon of Mariah Carey's voice. When the sound of the jingle bells comes in, I shimmy my shoulders to the beat. Christina covers her mouth with her hand, shoulders shaking. Don't ask me how, but I hit every single word in the first verse, and by the time the chorus comes, I'm belting out the lyrics to *All I Want for Christmas is You.*

Christina hunches forward with laughter, clutching her stomach, until she has tears in her eyes. She joins me for the last chorus, singing into the imaginary microphone in my hand, and when it's over, she claps with pride.

"That was amazing." She dabs the corners of her eyes. "One day, I'd like to hear you sing something for real."

One day.

Two simple words that hold so much weight.

For the remainder of the ride, one question sticks out in my mind: Will we see each other when this trip is over?

Six

Christina

"Welcome to the Hellmouth."

Jake raises an eyebrow. "Huh?"

I shake my head. "Nothing."

At least I could stake vampires in the Hellmouth. Keep them away with sunlight and garlic. But here, at my mother's winter home? No such luck.

Jake and I stare out the windshield at the two-story cabin. So many wonderful memories were created here when me and my sisters were kids. Snowball fights, watching movies by the fire, decorating the tree.

If only Christmas remained as magical as it was when we were children.

Jake gestures to the house. "I like the wrap-around porch."

"Mmm."

"You didn't tell me it was an *actual* log cabin. It's beautiful."

"Yeah."

He turns to face me, and takes my hands into his. "You're going to be okay, rainbow girl. We've got this. It's only a couple of days, and then we're out of here."

Why does that thought make my stomach churn even more?

I've been swept up into the whirlwind that is Jake Fallon. He went from the sexy-as-sin escort I thought he was, to a conniving liar, to something … more. All in the matter of twenty-four hours. With the truth out in the open, I should be leery of him. I shouldn't trust him. But Jake trusted me with his deepest, darkest secret, and bared his broken soul—and I felt the magnitude of that like an elephant sitting on my chest.

On top of everything, Jake is sweet, and respectful. He doesn't ask me to hide who I am. He makes me laugh. I haven't felt this spark of excitement since …

I don't think I've ever felt like this before.

Not even when I was engaged to the man I was supposed to spend my life with.

And maybe that was the problem. I did what I thought I was *supposed* to do. I did what made my mother happy, instead of what made me happy.

Staring into Jake's endless ocean eyes, I smile. "I'm happy you're here with me."

One corner of his mouth curves up. "Me too."

"You might not think so once we step inside that house. If you climb out a window, and run away, I won't hold it against you."

He chuckles. "You don't have any faith in me. I'll charm the pants off of everybody in there, you just wait and see."

I pat the top of his hand, and swing open the passenger door. "You might be a rock star, but unless you're Jesus Christ himself walking through that door, my mother won't care who you are."

He stills. "You don't think anyone will recognize me, do you?"

I laugh. "Pfft. No offense, but nobody in my family listens to rock music. According to Mom, it's the devil's music. And my sisters are into country."

He cringes, and mutters, "Country."

46

I revel in one last moment of quiet before I stomp the snow off my boots on the welcome mat. Jake clasps my hand, and gives it a squeeze. A light wisp of calm brushes down my spine. I inhale a shaky breath, and push open the door.

We're assaulted by sound.

Lots and lots of sound.

Children's feet stomp against the wooden floor upstairs, as they run from room to room shouting, "Whoa!" and, "Cool!" and, "Come see this!"

Pots clank in the kitchen, as my mother undoubtedly has begun preparing for our feast.

My sisters' high-pitched voices gush over Rachel's growing belly, while their husbands' slap palms and animatedly discuss football stats.

I haven't seen everyone since the spring. I visit for Easter and Christmas every year since I moved to Manhattan. They're together much more than I am, as they all live so close to one another. I feel the twinge of jealousy every now and then, but I remind myself that I was the one who wanted to leave. I had to put distance between us for my own mental health.

That doesn't mean I don't miss them like crazy.

Jake stays rooted to the floor, and it's my turn to give his hand a reassuring squeeze. It can be intimidating stepping into such a big, loud family.

We enter the kitchen, lingering in the doorway, and all conversation ceases.

One giant awkward record scratch.

"H-hi. Merry Christmas." My voice sounds meek and pathetic.

Jake holds up his palm, and flashing a dazzling smile. "Hi, everyone. I'm Jake. Thank you for having me this weekend."

Thank God I didn't tell anyone I was bringing someone named Dominick to dinner.

Mom's slate grey eyes zero in on Jake. "Of course. There's always room for another at our table. Even if it is last minute."

I flinch. "I'm sorry. I didn't think it was a big deal. We always make so much food."

47

Adelle, wraps her arms around me in a tight hug. "It's no problem at all. We're so happy you brought someone." She shakes Jake's hand. "I'm the oldest sister. Mess with Chrissy, and you'll have to mess with me."

My cheeks flush. "God, Adelle. That's not necessary."

She shrugs. "Better to let him know right off the bat."

"She's just looking out for her little sister." Jake pulls me to his side, and winks. "Nothing wrong with that."

Adelle beams.

I shake my head. "This is Adelle's husband, Jim. Their daughter, Mia, is running around somewhere."

Louise, my second-oldest sister steps forward, but a very pregnant Rachel pushes past her. "Hi, I'm Rachel. I'm Chrissy's favorite sister."

Louise smacks her arm. "Hey, I resent that. I thought I was the favorite sister. I'm the one who taught her how to drive."

Adelle plants her hands on her hips. "Hey, I thought I taught you how to drive, Chrissy."

Louise rolls her lips between her teeth. "Which is why I then had to teach her how to drive."

Adelle scoffs. "What's wrong with my driving?"

Jim massages her shoulders. "Nothing's wrong with your driving, sweetheart. You're a very safe driver."

Rachel snorts. "And by safe, he means slow."

Louise leans in while Adelle and Rachel bicker. "The boys are upstairs. Wait until you see how big Mason got."

I smile. "I can't wait to see them."

Mom moves across the kitchen until she's standing in front of Jake, sizing him up. "It's nice to meet you, Jake. I'll introduce myself since my daughter seems to have misplaced her manners. I'm Eleanor."

"I was going to introduce you," I mutter.

"Don't mumble, sweetheart. It's rude."

Jake grins. "I love it when she does that. She always makes me laugh."

Mom purses her lips. "Yes, she's quite the comedian, this one."

My stomach twists.

Great. Mom's already in a mood.

Jake greets Don, Louise's husband, and Michael, Rachel's husband, and they immediately get into a conversation about football.

Rachel grabs my wrist. "Where have you been hiding him?"

"You might want to get a napkin. You're drooling."

Her eyes roam over Jake's body, lingering on his sculpted arms. "He is a work of art. I'm impressed, little sister."

I bite back a smile. "How do you feel?"

"Like a baby beluga. Don't change the subject. Tell me more about this strapping young man you've brought home, and told me nothing about."

I pop a nonchalant shoulder, though I don't feel an ounce of nonchalance. "It's still new."

That was good, right? It's generic enough.

"Jake, we're putting you to work." Louise holds up a bag of sweet potatoes. "Peel, and dice."

He salutes her. "Yes, Captain."

"That's what I like to hear." She jabs her husband in his side. "You should start calling me Captain."

Don rolls his eyes, but there's no malice behind them. "Jake, you're making me look bad."

"I'm helping you out, man." Jake claps him on the back. "Your wife just gave you a very valuable piece of information. Use it to your advantage."

Louise beams up at Jake, and then sticks out her tongue at Don. "Happy wife, happy life, remember?"

Don chuckles, and places a chaste kiss on her forehead. "Yes, Captain."

Adelle snaps her fingers in front of my face. "Come on, Chrissy. Stop staring at your boyfriend, and get to work."

My cheeks flame, and I spin around. "I'll get started on the mushrooms."

Mom's curious gaze burns a hole in my back. I glance over my shoulder at her, and give her a tight smile.

What's going on in her head?

Does she know I'm lying?

Can she sense that something's up between us?

I pull out the drawer under the oven, and take out the largest cookie sheet.

Mom lowers herself into a stool at the island. "So, Jake. What do you do for a living?"

The pan slips from my fingers, and clatters to the floor with a loud bang.

"Jesus, Chrissy." Adelle picks it up, and hands it to me. "What's with you?"

My eyes dart to Jake, and back to my sister. "Sorry."

Jake clears his throat. "I'm an editor, like your daughter. We work together at Anchor Publishing."

Okay, that sounded believable.

Mom hums. "And how long have you worked there?"

My eyes widen. We didn't go over that!

"What are you writing an article for the Sunday paper?" A nervous laugh ripples out of me. "Does it matter how long he's worked there?"

Mom glares at me. "Don't be rude, Chrissy. It's a perfectly reasonable question. I'm just getting to know the boy."

Jake holds up a hand. "It's fine. I don't mind. I've worked there for almost six years now."

Rachel balks at me. "You've worked together for all this time, and you haven't told me about him?"

Louise rolls her eyes. "Does she ever tell us about anything? Chrissy is like Fort Knox when it comes to her glamorous life in the big city."

Mom titters, and presses Jake for more information. "Have you lived in New York your whole life?"

"Yes, ma'am. Born and raised."

Michael, gestures to Jake's forearm with his knife. "I like your tattoo. That must've hurt."

Jake shakes his head. "Not too bad. The outline was the worst part, but that was over within fifteen minutes."

Mom purses her lips. "I don't understand why anybody wants to mark themselves like that."

It's a discourteous comment, but Jake takes it in stride. "My mom isn't into tattoos either."

"Do you play guitar?" Michael asks.

I glance over at Jake's expression, but he shrugs like it's no big deal. "I used to play it a lot more when I was younger. Work has kept me busy."

Rachel smooths her palm over her round belly, wearing a mischievous smile as she flicks her eyes to mine. "I'm sure it has."

My stomach twists tighter with each question, waiting for the other shoe to drop. Will there be a question we can't answer with ease? Surely, my mother will come up with something outrageous.

"Take it easy over there, killer." Don chuckles, gesturing to my mushrooms. "You're going to chop your finger off if you're not careful."

I grimace, and loosen my grip on the knife.

Adelle plants her hand on her hip. "Seriously, Chrissy. We all know you don't want to be here, but you could at least act like you're having fun."

I scoff. "That's not true. I'm happy to be here with all of you."

Louise shakes her head. "Something's up with you. You're acting weird."

Mom's narrowed gaze rakes over me, as if she can see right through me.

"We had a long night trying to find a hotel in the snow," Jake says. "She's tired."

"You should've planned ahead." Mom shakes her head in disapproval. "You knew the weather would be bad."

"You're right." I drop my chin, and turn to rinse the mushrooms in the sink.

A warm hand snakes around my waist, and I jump.

"Relax, rainbow girl." Jake's raspy voice is soothing against my ear. "Everything's okay." He drops the knife into the sink, and presses his lips to my cheek before returning to the island.

The kitchen is silent, all eyes on me.

"Is it hot in here?" I lean over the sink, and yank open the window.

Rachel giggles under her breath. "Something's definitely hot in here."

My nephew, Mason, tears into the room. He stops in front of Jake, and points up at him. "You're a stranger."

Jake laughs, and kneels down. "My name is Jake. What's yours?"

"I'm Mason. I'm four, and I'm a big boy."

"Yes, you are. I like your T-Rex shirt. I used to love dinosaurs when I was a kid."

Warmth pools in my chest as I imagine what Jake was like as a child, before the depression.

Mason scoots closer to Jake, climbing onto his knee and using it as a chair. "Who's your favorite dinosaur?"

Jake taps his finger against his chin, and looks up at the ceiling. "Hmm. Probably Petrie."

Oh, my God. The rock and roll star watched *The Land Before Time*?

Mason's brows pinch together. "Who's Petrie?"

"He's a funny little pterodactyl from a movie. Have you ever seen *The Land Before Time*?"

Mason shakes his head, and looks up at his mom. "Can we watch it?"

Louise smiles. "Sure. We'll see if it's on Netflix tonight."

Mason hops down from Jake's lap, and trots over to me. "Aunt Chrissy, I like your boyfriend. He's better than the last one."

Then he zips out of the room.

Rachel lifts her water glass. "I second that."

Everyone laughs, but sadness pricks deep in my gut. Jake isn't my boyfriend. It's all an act.

Will I ever find someone like him for real?

When we finish preparing the fixings for dinner, Jake tugs on my elbow. "Why don't you give me a tour of the house, and show me where we're sleeping? I'll bring our bags up."

I lead Jake upstairs to the last room on the left. "Well, you've already won over Rachel."

His eyebrows lift. "What did I do?"

I squeeze his bicep. "You look like this, and she has pregnancy hormones."

He grins. "Tell me what's going on in that pretty head of yours. Everything seems to be going well so far."

I scrub my hands over my face, and rake them through my hair. "I'm just waiting for a question we can't answer, or for someone to realize we're lying—"

"They won't."

"And my mother's interrogating you like she's an FBI agent—"

"It's not that bad."

"And everyone keeps calling me Chrissy, even though I've told them for years how much I hate it—"

"I think it's cute."

"And you're captivating, and cool, and ridiculously sexy, and nobody like you would ever be interested in someone like me, so they're all wondering what you're doing—"

Jake's hands cup my face, and he walks me backward until my shoulders hit the wall. It happens so fast, and before I can ask what he's doing, his mouth is on mine.

Smooth and warm, his lips feel like butter melting against me. White-hot heat rips through me like a wildfire, and I'm helplessly consumed by it. I can't speak, can't think, can't do anything except be here in this moment.

I push up onto my toes, and slide my hands into his thick hair, gripping onto the silky strands. He parts my lips with his tongue, and I open for him, groaning as he dips inside, deepening the kiss. His large hands skim down my ribs, blazing a trail to my hips, and he sweeps me up into his strong arms. My legs wrap around his waist, and I arch my back, pressing my chest to his. Our kiss intensifies—an urgent, passionate, toe-curling kiss. We're desperate and frantic, panting and breathless, nipping and sucking until our lips are swollen.

I've never been kissed like this before.

And now, I don't want anything less than this level of explosiveness.

Jake Fallon just ruined me.

Jake Fallon, my fake boyfriend, who's only kissing me because …

Wait, no one else is around. Why is he kissing me?

"Jake," I murmur against his mouth.

"I know, rainbow girl."

God, I can't think straight when he calls me that.

"Jake, wait."

His body stills, and he lowers me to my feet. "What's wrong?"

"W-why … what was that for?"

"You were freaking out about us not being a believable couple, so I did what believable couples do. They kiss." He heaves a sigh, and disappointment slants his eyebrows. "Did I cross the line? Should I not have done that?"

I touch my fingertips to my throbbing lips, already missing the heat of his mouth. "I didn't mind it."

A laugh rumbles deep in his chest. "Good, because I can't promise that I won't do it again."

My knees buckle.

Please, do it again.

His head dips down, and he presses the softest kiss to my lips. "You're talking out loud again."

I squeeze my eyes shut, and bury my face in his chest.

Pounding on the door makes the both of us jump.

"Tour of the house, my ass," Rachel calls from the hallway. "Get out here. Mom's looking for you two."

I send a silent groan up to the clouds, and Jake clasps my hand. "Come on, Rainbow Brite. I've got you."

But for how long?

Seven

Jake

I'm hard as a rock at Christmas dinner.

I'd laugh if it weren't so painful.

That kiss with Christina has my head—and my dick—all sorts of messed up. The softness of her plump lips, the way her body felt wrapped around me, the whimpers and moans she made …

Fuck.

Christina leans in, and the sheer proximity of her lips has me breaking into a sweat. "You okay?"

I gulp down a few sips of water. "Yeah, why?"

She glances down at my hand on her thigh. "You're gripping me so hard, your knuckles are turning white."

I loosen my grip, and give her a sheepish grin. "Just making sure you don't bolt out of here."

She smiles, and drags her fingers up and down my arm. "I'm not going anywhere."

Something's different about her since we kissed. She's more relaxed, more comfortable. Not so jumpy and nervous like she was when we first arrived. She also hasn't taken her hands off me for one second. To an onlooker, the touches are innocent—totally PG. Nothing more than a couple showing their affection. But I feel every caress down to my core, as if she's touching my soul.

The way she looks up at me with those big brown eyes, it's like she sees me.

Me.

Not the depressed nutcase.

Not the persona I played on stage.

She sees me, and she's happy with what she sees. Proud, even. Proud to have me by her side. It's a foreign feeling for me. Sure, people have been proud of me, but that was only because I was making them money. When was the last time someone was satisfied with just me—without a guitar strapped around my neck?

I've only known Christina for two days, yet she's turning my whole world upside-down.

Christina's nephew, Louie, slumps down into his chair. He sniffles, and wipes his nose with the back of his hand.

"What's wrong, bud?" Christina asks.

He lifts his watery eyes to her. "Mia said there's no such thing as Santa."

The table grows quiet.

Mason's little nose wrinkles as he looks up at his big brother. "That's not true. Santa's real. He's coming tonight."

Louie shakes his head. "He's not coming. He's not real."

Adelle leans in, and scolds her daughter. "Why would you say that to him?"

Mia's bottom lip juts out. "He was teasing me, saying that Santa wasn't going to bring me any presents. He said I was getting coal."

Louise looks at her son. "Lou, is that true? Were you being mean to your cousin?"

He hikes a shoulder, and looks down at his lap.

I set my fork down, and dab the corner of my mouth with my napkin. "Sometimes people say things they don't mean when they're angry. Right, Mia?"

She looks to her mother, and then me. "Yeah, that's right."

"Why do they do that?" Louie asks.

"They feel hurt, so they want to lash out and make someone else feel the same way they do. So, they say something they know will upset them."

Mia nods, turning to her cousin. "You hurt my feelings when you said I wouldn't get any gifts from Santa."

Louie frowns. "I'm sorry, Mia. I didn't mean it. Santa's going to bring you lots of toys."

She smiles her toothy grin. "I'm sorry too."

Eleanor sits back against her chair. "Do you have any siblings, Jake?"

"No, ma'am. I'm an only child. My parents used to joke that I was such a handful, they couldn't have handled another kid running around the house."

"Where are your parents now? Why aren't you with them for the holidays?"

"Because he's with us." Christina's grip around her fork tightens.

Eleanor sets her glass down on the table. "I'm just trying to get to know your boyfriend, Chrissy."

"It's okay." I cover Christina's hand with mine. "My parents are snow birds. They live in Florida during the winter months, so I decided to spend this Christmas with Christina. Maybe next year, she'll come down with me to visit my family."

Eleanor quirks a brow. "You're planning next Christmas already."

It's a statement, not a question, so I smile, and stuff my mouth with a forkful of mashed potatoes.

Lying to Christina's family feels wrong, but it's better than telling them the truth.

Conversation continues around the table, but I'm acutely aware of Christina's every move. The way she leans into my touch, the way her chest rises and falls in short breaths when my fingers brush against her skin, the way her hand hasn't stopped touching me throughout the entire meal. Heat rolls off her like a boiling pot, and I want to push her until she bubbles over.

After dinner, Mason bolts out of his seat and over to me. "Mommy found *The Land Before Time* on Netflix. Can we watch it now, Jake?"

I smile. This kid is adorable with his pudgy cheeks, and wide blue eyes. "Sure, bud. I just have to help the adults clean up. Why don't you save me a spot on the couch?"

He nods as if I gave him the most important job, and runs into the living room.

Christina shakes her head, and slides her palm along my back. "You're full of surprises, Jake Fallon."

I lean down, and press my lips to her forehead. "Gotta keep you on your toes, rainbow girl."

Rachel takes my plate, and adds it to the stack in her hands. "Why do you call her rainbow girl?"

Christina's cheeks tinge a rosy pink, and I grin. "Because she wears bright colors."

"That's for sure," Adelle says with a snort. "You should've seen her growing up. Neon-colored tights, and big tutus. She'd mismatch everything, and wear stripes with polka dots."

Christina's mother hums in agreement. "Bright colors to match her bright personality."

The way she says it, she makes it clear that it isn't a compliment.

Christina's chin hits her chest, and her hair falls around her face.

Oh, hell no.

I wrap my arm around her waist, and tilt her face to bring her eyes back to me. "It's what attracted me to her. She lights up the room, and you can't help but be enchanted by her."

Christina's lips part in surprise.

Rachel squeals. "You two are the cutest. I can't even take it."

Everyone clears off the table, and Louise takes dish duty, shooing us out of the kitchen.

In the hallway, Christina pulls me aside, worrying her bottom lip between her teeth. "You're getting good at this whole pretending thing. You have everyone fooled."

Something tugs at my heart, and I'm overcome by the sudden urge to stamp that thought right out of her mind.

I cradle the back of her head, and claim her mouth. She immediately exhales, and melts against me, fisting my shirt in her small hands. I'm surrounded by her intoxicating scent of pineapple and coconuts. Our kiss is hungry, and her body trembles in my arms.

Does she feel this too?

Not sure what *this* is, but it's there between us.

I pull back, cutting the kiss short, and I look straight into her eyes. Seconds tick by in the narrow hallway, each of us standing there, panting and staring at one another.

"I'm not pretending." The words whoosh out of me, and I'm powerless to stop them.

But she's not smiling.

Maybe I read this all wrong.

Rein it in, you idiot. Slow down.

Mason's voice calls from the living room. "Jake? Where are you?"

Before she can say anything, I take Christina's hand in mine, and lead her into the next room.

Mason pats the cushion beside him, grinning from ear to ear in his Rudolph onesie pajamas.

Rachel hooks elbows with Christina. "I'm going to borrow her, if you don't mind. It looks like Mason wants you all to himself anyway."

I glance at Christina to make sure she's okay, and she nods, offering me a faint smile.

I spend the duration of the movie kicking myself for what I let slip in the hallway.

Why would someone like Christina be interested in a fuck up like me? She's the entire sun, and I'm just a dark cloud on a rainy day. What the hell am I doing here? This was a reckless decision, pretending to be someone I'm not, and then helping Christina lie to her whole family. Now I'm feeling things I shouldn't. I was doing fine keeping to myself, and drowning my sorrows at the bottom of a bottle every night. Yet here I am, craving the touch of this beautiful woman, excited over the prospect of holding her in my arms as she falls asleep later.

I'm so fucked.

Mason conks out in my lap before the end of the movie. When Christina and her sister return to the living room, Rachel shimmies her hips at the sight of her sleeping boy. "You can babysit any time, my friend." She scoops him up, and whisks him upstairs.

Christina lowers herself onto the couch beside me. "Have you ever heard of a White Elephant?"

Like the one sitting in the room between us right now?

I shake my head, toying with a strand of her hair.

"Every year, we buy a generic gift without a specific person in mind. Then, we each pick a number. Whoever chooses the number one goes first, and that person gets to select one of the wrapped gifts in the middle of the room. Whoever has two goes next, and that person has the option of stealing whatever the first person picked, or picking from the pile of gifts. Make sense?"

I rub my palms together. "Sounds ruthless. I love it."

She flashes me a devious smirk. "I bought two gifts, so one of them is from you."

"What did I buy?"

She leans in to whisper, "A bottle of wine."

I give her neck a gentle bite. "Thanks, rainbow girl."

Her eyelids flutter closed, and my favorite red color travels up her neck, and into her cheeks.

I love knowing I can affect her like this.

Adelle snaps her fingers as she enters the living room. "I'm going to have to separate you two if you can't keep your hands to yourselves."

Jim wraps his arm around her waist. "Don't spoil their fun. We used to be just like them when we were young and in love."

Love.

My stomach bottoms out, and Christina's hand freezes where she was just stroking my forearm.

"It's too soon for love," her mother says, as she sits in a recliner with a huff. "Their relationship is still new."

Louise waves a dismissive hand. "Pfft. Time has nothing to do with love. When you know, you know. Doesn't matter if it's the first day, or the tenth, or the hundredth."

"Please." Eleanor rolls her eyes. "Let's get this game started."

Christina steals a glance at me out of the corner of her eye. *Sorry,* she mouths.

I shoot her a wink, and rest my arm on her thigh.

Michael passes around a bowl with folded pieces of paper, and we each take one. Christina ends up with number two, and I get eight—the second-to-last one.

Jim whistles. "Beginner's luck."

"What can I say? I'm a lucky guy." I nuzzle Christina's cheek as I say it, and she giggles, giving me a playful shove.

Don selects the first gift, and unwraps a pair of waterproof winter gloves. "Hell, yeah!" He pumps his fist in the air.

Louise pats his knee. "Much better than the gift card to Victoria's Secret you won last year."

Christina's up next. She makes a beeline straight for a medi-um-sized gift bag with sparkly gold tissue paper. When she returns to her spot beside me, she reaches inside and pulls out a long silk scarf covered in bright watercolor butterflies.

Her eyes widen, and her lips part on a gasp. "Oh, my. This is beautiful."

"That's perfect for you." Rachel winks, revealing herself as the one who purchased it.

Everyone takes their turn, and no one steals anyone else's gift. Not even Rachel, who ends up with a bottle of wine that she can't drink.

She pats her belly. "I'll save this for when I give birth."

"Your turn, Jake." Eleanor waves her arm around the circle. "De-cide your fate: Steal one of our gifts, or choose one of the last mystery boxes."

I'm no fool. I go with one of the untouched boxes, and end up with an ice scraper.

Christina's mother rises from her chair, walking toward the re-maining gift on the floor. Then, she makes a quick left, and snatches Christina's scarf out of her hands.

Eleanor's eyes widen, Rachel gasps, and Christina drops her gaze to her empty lap.

Is this woman for real?

Irritation spikes in my veins.

"Steal it back," Rachel whispers.

But my rainbow girl shakes her head. "If Mom wants it, she can have it."

We watch as she takes the last gift from the center of the room, and opens a gas station gift card.

Oh, fuck no.

Rachel yawns. "This mama is heading to bed. My boys are going to get us up bright and early to see what Santa brought."

"Me too." Christina shoots up from the couch, and tugs my hand. "Come on."

"You go ahead. I'm going to stay and help your Mom clean up."

Her eyebrows pinch together as she nods.

Everyone shuffles upstairs to bed, but Louise hangs back. "Mom's rough on her. Always has been."

I ball up the torn pieces of wrapping paper. "Why is that?"

She shrugs. "Maybe because Chrissy's the most headstrong one out of us. She's a lot like Mom in that regard."

Yeah, right. Christina is nothing like her mother.

"You're good for her, Jake. She seems happy with you." Then she glares at me. "Don't mess it up."

I chuckle. "I'll try not to."

Eleanor returns to the living room with a black garbage bag. "I don't know why I even bother cleaning. This living room will look like a Christmas bomb went off in the morning."

I clear my throat, and muster some courage. "Can I ask you a question, Eleanor?"

She sets down the bag, and arches an impatient brow. "You're not going to ask for my daughter's hand in marriage, are you?"

I smirk. "No."

"Good."

I heave a sigh. "Christina has a lot of respect for you."

"That's not a question, Jake. Cut to the chase."

Fine. She wants me to be blunt? I can do blunt.

"Why did you take that scarf from her when you knew damn well that she wanted it?"

Her eyes widen, and her head jerks back. "Excuse me?"

I slip my hands into my pockets. "She loves you. She tries everything she can to please you. But her stomach has been in knots ever since we got into the car to come here yesterday. I tell her not to worry, and to just be herself—and back home, she is herself. She's smart, and funny, and caring. She's unlike any woman I've known. But it's you she's afraid to be herself around. And now I see why. You knew she liked that scarf, and you took it from her. Tell me, Eleanor: Do you even plan on wearing it? Or was it just something you could use against your daughter?"

She blanches, and sputters like a clucking chicken. "I can't believe you'd have the nerve to speak to me like this in my own house. You're a guest. How dare you question my relationship with my daughter."

"That doesn't answer my question."

Eleanor blinks, staring at me for several minutes. I think she's going to hand me my ass, but instead, she snatches the gift bag off the recliner, and shoves it against my chest. "It's just a scarf. This is ridiculous."

Then she spins around, and exits the room with a huff.

My parents might not understand the issues I've had, and we might not see eye-to-eye on everything ... but they'd never purposely try to snuff out my happiness.

I guess it takes another family's disfunction to help you appreciate your own.

I finish straightening up the living room, and set the garbage bag in the kitchen before heading up the stairs.

Rachel and I both jump when I round the corner, and find her skulking in the hallway.

"What are you doing?"

She gives me a sheepish grin. "Eavesdropping."

I cross my arms over my chest. "Enjoy the show?"

"Very much." She leans in. "No one's ever put my mother in her place like that. It was amazing to watch."

I pop a shoulder. "It's about time somebody did it. You guys should stick up for your sister more often."

She nods, smoothing a palm over her belly. "Was Chrissy really nervous about coming here?"

"Yup. Can't say I blame her."

A stream of air blows out of her nose. "I feel terrible."

"So do something about it." I give her shoulder a squeeze, and leave her standing in the hall.

Eight

Christina

I change into my pajamas, and fling myself onto my back in the middle of my bed.

I'm too tired from the events of the day to acknowledge the fact that my own mother stole the gorgeous scarf I had my sights set on. It's what she does. She sees a flash of happiness in my eyes, and then she puts it out.

I'll never understand her, and I've spent years trying to.

I stare up at the ceiling, waiting for Jake to return. I'll feel better when he's here. There's something about him that puts me at ease. That comforts me.

I'm not pretending. His words bounce off the walls in my mind.

What did he mean?

Why would he say that?

Of course, we're pretending. This whole thing we're doing is a plan I hatched. It's nothing more than a fake relationship.

Then why does it feel so real?

The bedroom door cracks open, and I can make out Jake's large shadow entering the room. He lowers himself onto the edge of the bed, and trails his fingers along my cheekbone. "Hi."

I smile, and scoot up against the headboard. "Hi."

He flicks on the lamp on my bedside table. "You okay?"

I blow out a long exhale through my lips. "It's been a long day."

"Maybe this will make you feel better." He sets a gift bag in my lap, with sparkly gold tissue paper poking out of the top.

My eyebrows dip down. "Isn't this ..."

"Open it."

I pull out the pretty silk scarf I almost won in the White Elephant exchange earlier. "I don't understand."

"I confronted your mom. I told her that what she did was wrong, and that she should reconsider giving you the scarf."

My mouth falls open. "Why did you do that? W-what did she say?"

"Because you deserved it." His gaze skates over my face. "She told me I had nerve talking to her that way. And I told her she had nerve taking her daughter's happiness. But I know that it's about what the scarf represents. Your individuality. Your light. The thing that makes you extraordinary. She shouldn't try to extinguish what she doesn't understand."

My voice wobbles. "What did she say?"

"Nothing." He shrugs. "She handed me the bag, and walked out of the room."

Tears threaten to spill over my lids. I glance down at the bright-colored butterflies on the silk fabric. "No one's ever stuck up for me like that before."

"Maybe it's time you started sticking up for yourself."

I can't put into words what this gesture means to me, and I'm scared to try, for fear of what my heart will reveal for this man I barely know.

But it feels like I do know him.

And what's more, it feels like he knows *me*.

I've spent years as the black sheep of my family. Years dating someone who treated me as if I was something to be ashamed of. Yet here I sit, in the lap of a man who wants to see every color of my rainbow.

He pulls my legs onto his lap, and pulls off my fuzzy Santa socks.

My head falls back as he digs his thumbs into the heel of my left foot. "You don't have to do that."

He rasps his husky laugh. "Don't have to. Want to."

His strong hands massage my feet, releasing the stress from the day.

"You're really good at this."

"I played guitar for over twenty years. These fingers are skilled."

I stifle a moan. "You're not kidding."

After he works on my feet for a glorious few minutes, his hands travel up to my calves, giving each leg his undivided attention.

"I should be the one giving you the massage after subjecting you to my family all day."

"It wasn't so bad, Rainbow Brite." He kneads the muscle just above my knee, sending goosebumps flying over my skin. "Besides, I'm a giver. I like to please."

His words skate over me like silk, and along with his sensual touch, it's a deadly combination.

He rubs his way up my thighs, and just as his fingers skim under the thin material of my cotton pajama shorts, he pulls away. "Turn over."

With my heart in my throat, I do as he commands, lying on my stomach on the comforter. His hands return to my legs, and I pray he can't feel me trembling with need.

A low groan rumbles in his throat as his hands move over the swell of my ass. "God damn," he mumbles.

Those delicious hands of his press into my lower back, and I release a sigh as they move higher. He shifts his legs onto either side of my hips, and straddles me as he works out the knots in my shoulders.

"Your shoulders are very tense, Christina."

"Yes." I don't even recognize my own voice. It's breathy and needy and *my God* does this feel so freaking good.

I peek over my shoulder for a glimpse of the gorgeous man rubbing his hands all over my body. His messy hair falls into his eyes, and the muscles in his arms pop. I have to bite my lip to keep my mouth from falling open, and drooling on the pillow.

Jake's eyes zero in on my mouth, and I can feel his hardness pressed against my ass. "You make me crazy when you bite that lip."

He sparks something inside me that I've never felt with anyone else. Sexy. Bold. Natural.

With Jake, I feel desired.

I can be exactly who I am, and I don't have to hide.

I arch my back. "Show me how crazy I make you."

He comes down on top of me, and his hot breath is on my neck. "You have no idea all the things I want to show you."

I reach behind me, and wrap my fingers around the back of his neck, bringing his mouth to mine. "Show me, Jake."

I'm being careless, and reckless, but right now, I want to throw caution to the wind.

I *need* to.

I need *him*.

Jake sucks my bottom lip into his mouth, and releases it with a pop. Then his tongue sweeps into my mouth, searching for mine. One hand slips into my hair, and he grips it in his fist, while his other hand slides between my stomach, and the mattress.

I'm bucking under him, begging for it, soaked before his fingertips graze the top of my panties.

He pauses there, waiting.

"Jake, please."

He glides his long, sexy fingers over my swollen clit, and I release a moan.

He grunts deep in his throat. "As much as I hate to say this, you have to be quiet, baby. Don't want anyone to hear."

"Screw them," I whisper, grinding my hips against his hand.

His laugh vibrates against my skin. He nudges my legs apart with his knee. "Spread these pretty thighs wider for me."

Face down on the mattress, I edge up onto my knees, completely open for him. Jake brushes my hair away from my face, and drags his tongue along my neck.

Skilled doesn't even begin to describe him. His talented fingers strum through my folds with unerring precision, as if he knows what I need, where I need it, and exactly how I like it. His gentle strokes are a light torture that have me chasing his touch, rocking against him like a wild woman unchained.

"I want to taste you, rainbow girl." He bites my earlobe. "Will you let me?"

My eyes pop open, and my body stills. No one has asked me for that. My ex wasn't into it, unless he was on the receiving end. And now, someone who's had more experience than I could ever imagine is asking me to ...

"I-if you want to," is all I can manage to say.

"I want to." He rolls his hips against me, showing me how badly he wants it by the bulge in his pants. "But only if *you* want me to. This is all about you."

I meet his hungry gaze, and give him an infallible nod. "Yes, Jake."

He places a sweet kiss on my lips. "Stay just like this." He scoots down the bed, and peels my shorts and panties down to my knees in one fluid motion.

The air feels cool against my most sensitive spot, slick and wet with need. Butterflies in my stomach clamor in anticipation as Jake's head lowers behind me.

"Jesus," he murmurs. "So fucking perfect." He trails kisses along the curve of my ass, leading closer and closer to the inside of my thigh.

And then I feel his velvety, warm tongue on me.

He drags it over my seam, languid and slow, like he's savoring every drop. He swirls his tongue around my clit, and then slides his tongue all the way back to do it again.

An explosion of pleasure ripples through me, igniting every cell in my body. On my knees, baring myself to him, I should feel vulnerable and exposed. But I've never felt more powerful. He's serving me. Worshiping my body the way it deserves.

The way *I* deserve.

I melt on his mouth, pushing against the hot wet glide of his tongue, begging him in nonsensical clips of *yes*, and *please*, and *more*. He groans like a starved man indulging at a feast, and I wish I could see the expression on his face. Watch as he laps me up, and brings me to the brink of ecstasy.

I come undone, and bury my cries into the pillow as shivers rack through my body.

This is unlike anything I've ever felt, and I want it every day. Every. Day.

I collapse onto my stomach, and Jake pulls me to his side. I wrap my arms and legs around him, nuzzling my head into the crook of his neck, and breathe in his sweet and spicy scent.

In his embrace, I'm warm and sated. And I'm happier than I've been in a long time.

We lie there in quiet bliss, and within seconds, I drift off listening to the steady rhythm of his breaths.

When my eyes open again, darkness blankets the room. My fingers skim over cold sheets beside me, and I squint at the alarm clock on the nightstand.

Midnight.

I wrap the comforter around my body, and shuffle over to the glass doors leading to the balcony.

"What are you doing out here?"

"Couldn't sleep." Jake turns to me with a half-smile, and reaches for me, pulling me into his lap on the wooden chair. "Merry Christmas."

I brush my fingers through his hair, searching his emerald eyes for more. "Merry Christmas."

"How old were you when you stopped believing in Santa?"

"I was young. First grade, maybe? I have three older sisters, so it wasn't easy keeping secrets in our house."

He nods, casting his gaze over the railing at the trees surrounding the cabin. "I found out in third grade. One of my friends told me. I was devastated. I asked my mom why she lied to me, why she let me believe such a ridiculous thing. She said, *We lie in order to keep the magic alive.* I didn't get it at the time."

"And now?"

His breath condenses into a grey cloud with his exhale. "And now, I wish I could go back to that lie. Everything was magical. Nothing seemed impossible. I was filled with happiness, and hope for the future."

My heart aches for him. "Does your depression get worse during the holidays?"

"It does." He focuses on a strand of my hair as he twirls it around his index finger. "But being here, with you, I feel a spark of that magic again."

Something warm spills in my chest, pooling, and spreading over me. "I don't know much about depression, but I know what it's like to feel sadness, and heartache. To feel as if some things are hopeless, no matter how hard you try. To wonder if you'll ever find the thing, or the person, meant just for you. To walk around this earth like a shell of yourself, too afraid to rise up, and speak your mind. Trying so hard to blend in, and be normal for once." I cradle his face in my hands, bringing his eyes to mine. "But I also know that those feelings don't last forever. Things change. We change."

He presses his lips to mine, the softest whisper of a touch. "You should never try to blend in, rainbow girl."

"Neither should you. You're not the only one who's gone through a tough time. You're definitely not the only one suffering with depression. And you're not the only celebrity who went down a bad path. Just look at Justin Bieber. He went from an adorable kid to a reckless jackass—and now, he's back on top and everyone loves him."

He lifts an eyebrow. "You're comparing me to Bieber?"

"It's the point, not the person."

His deep laugh rumbles in his chest. "You're right. But it's been difficult losing touch with my friends, and family. I don't know how to get back to where we were."

"Maybe you don't want to get back there. Maybe you need to get to higher ground instead."

He blinks, a confounded expression on his face.

I nudge him with my cold nose. "Let's go to bed."

Jake carries me back inside, and we fall asleep wrapped in each other's arms.

Nine

Jake

"**B**lue forty-two! Blue forty-two! Hut!"

My boots crunch against the snow as I charge toward the makeshift endzone. Michael launches the ball, and I jump to catch it. I glance over my shoulder, and grin.

Christina is hot on my heels, wearing that bright yellow hat, gritting her teeth as she pumps her legs to catch up to me.

I run faster.

She'd hate it if I slowed down to let her win.

How I know that, I'm not sure, but I just do.

Michael pumps his fist in the air. "Touchdown, baby!"

Christina jumps into my arms, and I let her tackle me to the ground. The snow is cold, but I don't feel a thing with this beautiful woman straddling me. I've been running hot all day with thoughts of last night replaying in my mind.

God, the way she bent over and spread herself for me ... the taste of her sweetness on my tongue ...

I break into a cold sweat, and an involuntary shiver ripples through my body.

Christina blushes. "Really?"

"Really." I grip her hips as best as I can in her big coat, and thrust my hips upward.

Her eyes heat, and a small gasp leaves her pretty lips.

I love that I can see every emotion, every thought, flash across her face.

And I love that I'm the one who can bring it out of her.

Learning that no man has made her feel the way I did last night released this ridiculous possessive caveman inside me. I want to be all of her firsts. Not to claim her, or stifle her, but to set her fucking free. I want to show her how good sex can be. I want to show her how every inch of her body should be adored. I want to show her that she should never accept anything less than exactly what she wants.

I want to be the one to do all of that for her.

And more than anything, I want her to trust me to do it.

Christina smacks my chest. "Get your head out of the gutter, rocker boy. I'm on offense this time, and I'm going to run circles around you."

I hoist myself up with her in my arms, and she squeals as I swing her in a circle before setting her on her feet. "Let's see what you got, rainbow girl."

Don takes quarterback position, and Christina bends forward, ready to run down field.

"Hut, hut!"

Christina and I take off in the same direction, and I'll give it to her, she's fast. But my legs are longer, and I catch up to her in a few strides. She growls when she spots me, and darts to the right. Don passes the ball, and we run for it as it sails through the air.

I'm all over her, blocking any chance she has at catching the ball.

She looks up at me and whispers, "I want your cock in my mouth later."

My arms go limp at my sides, and my jaw drops. "What?"

Then she jumps up, catches the football, and runs into the endzone for a touchdown.

That little devil.

Michael throws his hands in the air. "What the hell, man? Why'd you let her win? That was an easy interception."

I blink, clearing my vision of dirty, dirty thoughts. "Your sister-in-law is evil."

Christina throws her head back and laughs. "Who, me? Whatever do you mean?"

With a growl, I stalk over to her. She tries to run, but I hoist her over my shoulder. "Hey, kids. Who wants to throw snowballs at your Aunt Christina?"

Mia, Mason, and Louie cheer.

"There are only two rules. Rule number one." I hold up my index finger. "No head shots."

Louie nods. "What's rule number two?"

I flip Christina onto her back in the snow. "No mercy!"

The snowballs start flying, and Christina howls with laughter as she scrambles to her feet to get away. Rachel, Michael, Adelle, and Jim join in, while Louise yells at everyone to be careful from the sliding glass door to the cabin.

The kids get Christina good, but then the adults turn on them. Poor Mason can't get his snow into a ball, and he grows frustrated as he throws handfuls of powder into the wind.

Christina scoops him up, and they hide behind a tree. He watches her with wide eyes as she forms a ball of snow in his tiny hands, showing him how to pack it together. He tries on his own, and throws his arms around her when he tosses his first snowball. Her smile is so bright, and her eyes sparkle as she squeezes hew nephew tight.

Warmth seeps into my chest.

"You're totally gone for her, aren't you?"

I turn to my right, and find Rachel standing beside me. "What?"

She smiles. "The way you look at her, it's obvious."

"And how do I look at her?"

"Like she's the best thing you've ever seen, and you're scared shitless to lose her."

My heart thunders in my chest, and I swallow hard.

Rachel rests her hand on my shoulder. "In case she hasn't told you yet, she's crazy about you too." She winks, and heads back to the snowball fight.

Did Christina tell Rachel how she feels about me, or is Rachel just speculating?

Either way, Rachel is right: I *am* scared shitless to lose her.

The end of this trip is looming over us, and as much as I try to push it from my mind, I can't stop thinking about it.

Eleanor's voice cuts through my thoughts. "Come inside before you all catch a cold. Lunch is on the table."

Everyone takes off for the cabin, and Christina wraps her mitten around my hand.

"I'm not really hungry," I say. "Mind if I skip lunch, and get cleaned up?"

"Sure." She looks up at me with wide eyes. "Are you okay?"

I nod, and press a kiss to her forehead. "Just need a hot shower."

When I get to the bathroom, I toss my clothes onto the floor, and step inside the steamy glass shower. Pins and needles prick my frozen fingertips. I close my eyes, and try to relax under the hot spray of the water.

What if Christina doesn't want to see each other when we get back to New York?

Or what if she does?

What do I have to offer someone like her?

I'm not the talented, successful man I used to be. I have money, but she makes her own. She's not interested in that. She wants more.

Am I capable of giving her what she deserves?

Am I capable of love, and happiness?

Her pretty face flashes in my head. Long, silky hair. Innocent doe eyes. Luscious lips. Sinful curves. I see her yellow hat, and oversized coat. I see her bright wardrobe. And then I see her beautiful heart. So honest, and genuine, and selfless, and caring.

My lungs constrict, and realization settles in.

I'll try like hell to be what she deserves.

A noise draws my attention. Peeking my head outside the fogged-up shower door, my eyes pop with surprise.

Christina steps out of her jeans, and then pulls her sweater over her head. My dick hardens instantly at the sight of her pink bra and matching panties against her creamy skin. Her chest heaves, straining against the lace.

"If I would've known you were wearing that all day, I wouldn't have been able to concentrate on anything."

She smiles, but it disappears just as quick. With her gaze locked on mine, she reaches behind her back, and unclasps her bra. I hold my breath as she slides the straps down each shoulder, painfully slow, down her arms, until she lets it fall at her feet.

I know I'm gawking at her like a teenage boy, but I can't tear my eyes away. Full, round, perfect tits, with pink pert nipples, rise and fall with each shallow breath she takes. She bites her bottom lip, and I groan.

"You're gorgeous." My voice is hoarse, and I can barely get the words out. "Fucking stunning."

A rush of red steals up her neck, into her cheeks, and finally, *finally*, I get to see just how far down that red reaches. I want to follow the trail in between her breasts with my tongue.

Her thumbs hook into each side of her panties, and she drags them down her legs. When she steps out of them, she returns her eyes to mine, and waits. She's letting me get a good look at her, my brave girl.

"Can I join you?"

I huff out a laugh. "If you don't, I think I'd cry."

She grins, and steps inside the small shower with me. The air around us is electric, charged with anticipation. I don't know what her plan is, but even if we do nothing more than kiss, this will still go down as the sexiest encounter I've had.

Her eyes roam over my body, not stopping on any particular spot for too long, just taking it all in. Then, her hands come out to touch me. I hold still, letting her explore, over my shoulders, my chest, and the ridges of my abs. Her breath hitches as her thumbs trace my hip bones, leading down to where I'm pulsing for her, long and hard.

I clench my fists at my sides, digging my fingers into my palms so that I don't reach out for her and break this moment.

This moment is hers to do whatever she wants with it.

Wherever she leads, I'll follow.

"I wasn't joking, you know." She lowers herself onto her knees, her mouth hovering in front of my dick. She flicks her eyes up to mine, and the sight of her gazing up at me on her knees is almost too much to handle. "I want you in my mouth."

My dick twitches. "You don't have to."

She smirks, and uses my own words against me. "Don't have to. Want to."

Before I can utter another word, she grips the base of my cock in her soft hand, and sucks me into her mouth.

"Oh, fuck." My hand flies to the back of her head, tangling my fingers in her damp hair.

She keeps her eyes locked on mine as she glides me in and out of her mouth. Her tongue swirls over my crown, and I shudder, my hips thrusting forward a fraction of an inch before I rein myself in.

But Christina moans, taking me deeper this time. She takes my fist clenched at my side, and places it on the back of her head to join my other hand. "Show me how you like it, Jake."

My heart cracks open.

All the way open.

She's not some groupie, only interested in checking me off her list of accomplishments. She's not using me for her own personal gain.

No one's around to see.

This isn't part of some performance.

She wants to do this for me, the same way I wanted to do it for her last night.

"Fuck, Christina." I rock forward again. "You. Your mouth on me. That's how I like it."

Doesn't matter what she does.

She lets out a pleased hum, and pushes me as far back into her throat as she can handle. She scrapes her nails up my thighs, and lifts one hand to cup my balls, giving them a squeeze. She's so damn sexy the way she watches me. She wants to please me, to be what I want.

I want to be hers.

I grip her hair tighter, and lose myself in the rhythm of her mouth, dragging me out, and pulling me in, again, and again. It's too much. She feels too good.

"Christina, I'm going to come."

I expect her to release me with a pop, but she wraps her tongue around my dick and sucks me until I'm pulsing down her throat. My groans echo off the shower walls, and pleasure rips through me. I see stars. Bright, hot white light.

Then I see her.

Just her.

Be mine, I want to say.

Let's forget the act, and do this for real.

But instead, I hold her close.

We'll have plenty of time to talk on the drive home tomorrow.

We wash each other in silence, letting our hands caress and roam, learning the dips and curves of each other's bodies. It's sensual, and intimate, and I love every second of it.

As we're toweling off, Christina's phone buzzes on the floor where she left her jeans.

She smiles when she sees who's calling. "It's Miles. He's probably dying to know how it's going here."

"Talk to him. I'll go spend some time with your family so they don't suspect we're up to no good in here."

She arches an eyebrow, and bites her bottom lip.

My dick twitches back to life, and I shake my head. "You're going to kill me, woman."

She winks as she swipes her thumb across her phone. "Hey, Miles. Merry Christmas."

Back in the bedroom, I throw on a pair of jeans and a T-shirt. I walk over to the dresser, and when I reach for my bottle of cologne, my phone dings with a notification.

Trent: Hey, man. Been a while. Just wanted to wish you a Merry Christmas. Thinking about you. Hope everything is going all right.

I scrub a hand over my jaw, and stare at the text in disbelief. I haven't talked to Trent in months, but here he is reaching out. Hope buds in the pit of my stomach. My thumbs fly over the screen as I tap out a response, and hit *Send*.

Me: It's good to hear from you. Been thinking about you too. Hope Laura and the kids are doing well. Merry Christmas. Let's get together after the holidays.

Wearing a splitting grin on my face, I take my phone to show Christina. I know she'll understand how much this means to me, and I want to share it with her.

Her laughter floats through the closed door as I approach, and before I knock, I lean in to catch what she's saying.

She sighs. "I don't know, Miles. We're pretending to be together for my family."

The smile drops from my face.

She's quiet, and then responds to whatever Miles said. "Well, if I'm never going to see him again, I might as well have fun while I can."

I back away from the door as if I've been slapped.

Never going to see me again?

Wow.

I'm a fucking idiot.

Ten

Christina

I'm in trouble.

I tried playing it cool to Miles on the phone earlier, and he saw right through me—even from three hours away.

"You like him, baby girl. You *like* like him," he said.

Glancing up from my plate, my gaze finds Jake. He chose to sit across from me during dinner, which gives me the perfect view. He's chatting with my brothers-in-law as if he's known them forever, and he played Mason's animal guessing game for six rounds without one complaint—even when Mason's animal kept changing, and he had no idea what it ate, or where it lived, or if it had a tail. Jake just smiled, and encouraged him to continue.

Yeah, I *like* like him.

The past couple of days have been incredible.

But right now, something's off.

He's barely looked at me, or said one word to me since we left the shower.

Was I not good?

Did I do something wrong?

He seemed like he enjoyed it.

Doubt creeps in, like it always does, and I kick myself for it. I used to be bursting with confidence. But when you get cheated on, it does something to your mindset. You second-guess yourself, and compare yourself to others.

Jake was used to women throwing themselves at him for a long time. Though he's not famous anymore, he's still just as gorgeous. He could get anyone he wants. Why would he want me?

Because he thinks you're special.

I stretch my foot under the table, and rub against his ankle. His eyes flick to mine, but instead of smiling, or winking, or smirking—or any of the other things he's done during our trip—his lips press into a firm line, and he looks away.

My chest rises as I take a cleansing breath. Maybe he's just tired. He's been through a lot being here with my entire family.

And that's what I keep telling the nagging voice in my head.

When we finish dinner, Adelle sets the Monopoly box in the middle of the table. "Who's ready to lose?"

Rachel stifles a groan. "This is the worst game invented in the history of mankind. It's not even a game. They should've just called it *Adulting Sucks.*"

Everyone chimes in, taking their stance on the matter.

I tug Jake's elbow, pulling him to the side. "Hey, can I talk to you?"

He shrugs as if he couldn't care less.

Something's definitely wrong.

I lead him up the stairs, and into my bedroom. He closes the door behind him, and leans against it, eyes trained on the floor.

I take a step toward him, reaching out to touch his arm. "Is everything okay? You seem a bit off."

A humorless laugh escapes him, and he shakes his head, still not making eye-contact. "Yeah, Christina. Everything's fine."

Christina. No more rainbow girl, or Rainbow Brite.

"W-why don't I believe you?"

"I don't know. Hard to believe anything in this situation we're in."

His harsh tone has me stepping back. "What's that supposed to mean?"

He shoves his hand through his hair, and blows out an irritated breath. "Nothing. Let's just go play Monopoly and get this night over with."

Hurt stings my chest. "Okay, we're not going anywhere until you talk to me. Did I do something wrong? Say something wrong?" I pause, cringing. "Was I not good at ... what we did in the shower?"

Remorse flashes in his eyes, but only for a brief moment before his stony expression returns. "You were fine. That's not it."

"Oh, goodie. I was *fine*. Just what every girl wants to hear."

His jaw pops. "Why do you care anyway? This isn't real. We're just pretending."

Just pretending.

Tears prick my eyes. "What happened, Jake? Did my mother say something to you? You're not acting like yourself."

"Well, I guess we don't know each other as well as we thought we did." His eyes harden. "I'm playing my part until we go back to our normal lives. I'm just the escort you hired."

Anger blinds me until all I can see is red. "Fine. You want to be the escort?" I stalk over to the dresser, and dig through my purse. I pull out the envelope I'd put in there the night we left to come to Connecticut. "Here. Take your payment."

I fling the envelope, and fifty-dollar bills fan out around him. I storm out of the room. The picture frames hanging along the wall in the hallway rattle with the force of my slam.

When I get to the bottom of the stairs, I run straight into my mother, almost knocking her over.

"Honestly, Chrissy. What in God's name is wrong with you? Why are you behaving this way?"

My blood boils over. "Sorry I'm not perfect like you, Mom. I know how disappointing that must be for you."

Her head rears back. "You watch your snarky tone when you're in my house."

"Oh, I don't plan on staying in this house for one second longer." I shoulder past her, and stomp to the front door.

"Chrissy, wait." Louise steps in front of me. "Don't leave."

"Let her go." Mom crosses her arms over her chest. "It's what she does best. Just like her father."

I'm frozen where I stand, struggling to breathe, as if I've been sucker-punched in the gut.

"Mom!" Rachel steps into the living room. "How could you say something like that?"

Mom glares at me. "It's the truth, isn't it? She can't stand to be around us. That's why she never calls or visits."

Rage churns like a storm in my stomach. "You're the reason I never call or visit. You. You did this."

Louise grasps my forearm. "Stop. It's Christmas."

I bark out a laugh. "You're right. It *is* Christmas. The time for giving. Thanks for the scarf, Mom. It's so sad that my boyfriend had to beg you to give it to me."

She rolls her eyes. "You're acting crazy over a scarf."

"It's not just the scarf!" My voice echoes off the high ceiling. "You're never happy for me. Or with me, for that matter. Nothing I do is good enough for you."

"You're being dramatic."

"Do not diminish what I feel by calling me dramatic." I spread my arms out wide, and the words I've been holding in for years come tumbling out. "Admit it: You can't stand to see me happy because it reminds you of the life you never had. Dad left, and you punished us for it. You never wanted to see us succeed because you knew we'd leave you, and you'd be all alone."

She huffs out a bitter laugh. "Your sisters are happy. Husbands, and kids. They didn't leave. They stayed by my side because they appreciate the sacrifices I've made."

"I've always appreciated everything you've done. I've always respected you, and the person you are. But you can't give me that same respect in return. You put me down instead of letting me find my own way, and be who I am."

She shakes her head. "You and your father are lost souls. Nothing will make you happy. That's why Nick looked elsewhere. And in time, this new boyfriend of yours will too."

Tears stream down my cheeks.

"Mom, enough." Rachel points her finger in her face. "She's your daughter. You're going to regret saying these things to her."

"It's me. It's always me. Because it can't possibly be you." I wipe my eyes with the backs of my hands. "You never want to admit to your own flaws, which is sad because everyone has them. No one's perfect, but you hold them up to this impossible standard. It's exhausting. That's your biggest problem. And that's why Dad left."

I spin around, and walk out of the house.

I don't have my car, nor do I have Jake's keys to the Escalade—and I'm not wearing a coat. But it doesn't matter. Freezing to death in a snowbank would feel better than staying in that house getting carved up by my mother's sharp words.

So I trudge through the snow to clear my head. The wind whips the snow around me, making it hard to breathe, and even harder to see. I wrap my arms around my midsection as shivers rack through my body.

This was foolish.

So, so foolish.

Why did I think hiring a fake boyfriend would solve my problem? Nothing satisfies my mother. Her problem doesn't lie with who I date—her problem is with me. And I'll never be able to change that.

Headlights cut through the darkness. The snow crunches under tires as they roll alongside me.

"Get in."

I glare in the direction of Jake's deep voice, though I can barely make out his face through the falling snow.

"Come on, Christina. It's freezing."

Yes, yes it is.

"I have your jacket."

A jacket would be nice right about now.

85

"And your yellow hat."

I love that hat.

"Yellow mittens too."

I've lost all feeling in my fingers.

I growl. "Fine. But I'm only getting in because I don't want to get hypothermia."

I hop into the passenger seat, and Jake wraps my coat around my shoulders. I shove my hands into my mittens, and pull my hat over my head. The heat is cranked up high, so I huddle in front of the vent.

"Where were you walking to?"

I shrug. "Away."

"I heard the fight you had with your mom. Are you okay?"

I cut him a sideways glance. "You don't have to pretend to care."

He stops the truck, and shifts it into park. "I do care, Christina."

"Really? Thought you just wanted to get this night over with so we can go back to our normal lives tomorrow." I slump back against the seat, and cross my arms, staring out at the snow as it pelts the windshield.

"That's not ..." He sighs. "That's not what I want. I just said that because it's what you wanted."

My head whips around to look at him. "Why would you think that?"

His eyes slam closed, and when he opens them again, emotion burns in the intensity of his gaze. "I heard what you said to Miles on the phone."

Confusion pinches my features. "Wait, what? You were eaves-dropping on my conversation when I was in the bathroom?"

"It wasn't on purpose. I wanted to tell you something, and when I went to knock on the door, I heard you say that you didn't plan on seeing me once we got back to New York."

That's *why he was acting so cold.*

"Jake, you misunderstood what I was saying."

He levels me with a look. "I heard you, loud and clear. What's not to understand?"

"I was telling Miles about you—about how amazing you are, and about how much I've enjoyed our time together this weekend. He said it sounded a little too soon to be feeling this way for someone I barely know. He asked how I'd feel if you said you didn't want to see me again after our trip was over, and I said I wanted to stay in the moment, and have fun for as long as it lasted." I frown, and look down at my mittens in my lap. "He's very protective over me. He was the one who picked up my pieces when my engagement imploded. I know he means well, and he's looking out for me. But what you heard me say was only a reaction to what he was saying. It's not a reflection of the way I feel."

Jake's eyes soften. "And how is it that you feel?"

My heart beats a drumline in my chest.

I'm scared of putting myself out there.

Of getting my heart stomped on.

Of getting betrayed again.

But I can't let what happened in the past dictate the way the rest of my future will go. If I don't take this chance with Jake, then I'll never know what could've been.

I lift my chin, and suck in a brave breath. "We might only know each other for a couple of days, but I feel closer to you in days than I've felt with anyone I dated in months. You understand me. You like me the way I am, quirks and all. You don't make me feel like I'm not good enough, or like I have to change who I am." A lone tear slides down my cheek. "My own mother hasn't shown me that kind of acceptance."

Jake leans over the center console, and cups my face with his large hands. "That's your mother's loss. She gets to miss out on the extraordinary person you are."

I pull off each mitten, and cover Jake's hands with mine. "I'm sorry you thought I had no intention of seeing you after this weekend."

"I'm sorry I acted like such a dick tonight." He touches his forehead to mine. "I like you a lot. The thought of never seeing you again really bothered me."

"I was worried I wasn't as experienced as you wanted me to be."

He pulls back just far enough to look into my eyes. "You are perfect exactly how you are. You turn me on with just a kiss. And what happened in that shower today?" His eyes close, and his Adam's apple bobs. "I'm hard just thinking about it."

I grin, and climb over the console, straddling him in the driver's seat.

His arms wrap around my waist as he brushes his lips against mine. "I care about you, rainbow girl."

My nickname on his lips makes everything feel right again.

"I care about you too."

And then we spend the next hour kissing our worries and doubts away.

When we arrive back at the cabin, my mother is the only one still up.

I'd like to think she's waiting up for me, but that'd be asking a lot from her.

She glances up from the book she's reading. "Oh, good. You found her."

Jake smiles. "Told you I wouldn't let her get far."

I reach up and press a chaste kiss to Jake's cheek. "Can you give us a minute? I'll meet you upstairs."

He winks, and I lower myself onto the couch facing my mother.

Several quiet seconds pass between us.

Guess I'll start.

But Mom starts talking before I can get the words out. "I loved your father very much, you know."

I lean back against the cushion, and listen with rapt attention.

"He was the yin to my yang, as they call it. I was serious, and conservative. He was a jokester who didn't take life too seriously. He was full of life, and adventure. He loosened me up. Made me a better person." She places her book face-down on her lap. "Then he left, and he took all the light with him. I didn't see it coming. I racked my brain for years. Why did he leave? Why didn't I know something was wrong? And I see so much of him in you. I know it's not your fault. All kids have qualities from their parents. But I worry about you. About the life you're going to have."

"Why?" I interrupt. "What's so horrible about my life? I have a wonderful job that I love. I live in a safe neighborhood in the city that I love. I have friends. And most importantly, I love myself. Do you know how hard it was for me growing up knowing you didn't approve of anything I said or did? Or how hard it was to be engaged to someone who I didn't love—someone I was with just to make *you* happy? Yet I love myself in spite of it all. In spite of you."

"I just want you to live a good life. Get married, have kids. Be surrounded by your family."

"You want me to live *your* life. But I might not get married. I might not have kids. I don't have a plan, and that's okay. It doesn't make my life any less than yours, or any less filled with happiness and love."

She nods as if she understands. "You look happy."

For the first time in a long time, I feel at peace with myself.

"I am." I shrug. "I just wish you could be happy for me."

She stares at me, her slate grey eyes searching my face. "I'd like to try to be a better mother. If it's not too late. I don't want you to hate me."

"I don't hate you, Mom." I kneel onto the floor beside her chair, and clasp her hands. "I love you, and I appreciate everything you've sacrificed for this family. Just know that I'm not like Dad in one very important regard: I'll never turn my back on my family."

She sniffles, and glances away. "I'm sorry for the things I said to you tonight."

"Me too."

Mom lifts my hands to her lips. "Get to bed. Your boyfriend is waiting."

A small smile tugs at the corners of my mouth. "He's a good one, Mom."

"Yeah, I think he is."

I head upstairs lighter than I've felt this whole weekend.

Jake's face is illuminated by his phone screen in the dark bedroom. "How did it go?"

"It went better than expected." I toss my clothes into a heap on the floor, and slip into my pajamas. "I don't know if we'll ever understand each other, but we agreed to disagree, and she agreed to respect my differences."

"I'm so happy to hear that." He pats the mattress beside him. "Want to tell me about it?"

I shake my head, and slide under the covers. "I need to compartmentalize first. What are you looking at?"

He wraps an arm around my shoulders, pulling me close. "I want to show you something."

I take his phone, and read through a series of texts between him and Trent. "Oh, my God. This is your best friend, right?"

"Yeah, it is. He reached out today."

"Jake, that's great. And you're talking now?"

He nods. "A few days ago, I wouldn't have answered him. That's what I did. I pushed people away because it was easier." He kisses my forehead. "But opening up to you about what happened made me realize that I should be able to talk about it with the people who are important to me. I've missed having him in my life."

"I'm so proud of you." I smooth my fingers through his hair. "That takes courage."

He sets his phone down on the nightstand, and I curl myself around him, entwining our legs. We both let out contented sighs.

"I've been thinking about how we kind of did this all backwards. We went straight to living together, and meeting the family, before we've even had a proper date."

I prop my head up with my hand. "You want to take me on a date?"

He groans. "I wish the light were on so I could see that pink blush on your cheeks."

"How do you know I'm blushing?"

"I just do." He kisses the tip of my nose before reaching over and flipping on the lamp. "Ah, see? My favorite color."

"How is this tattooed, bad boy, rock god so damn sweet?"

He grins. "Not a rock god, but you can call me that any time you want."

"Speaking of ..." I chew my bottom lip. "Can you show me a video of you playing the guitar? You can pick the song. I just want to see you perform."

He reaches for his phone, and then pauses. "I'm not that same guy anymore."

I cup his face, and force his eyes to mine. "He's just one part of you. He's the talent you were blessed with. He's not *all* that you are."

Jake covers my hand with his, his intense green eyes slicing through the darkness. "I'm so glad I found you, rainbow girl."

"I guess it's a good thing I looked for an escort."

Jake laughs, and then he presses the softest kiss to my lips.

Eleven

Jake

The drive back to New York the next day is bittersweet.

The stress of this whirlwind trip is over, yet so is my undivided time with Christina. Going back to the real world fills my head with doubt, and questions. Christina has made it clear that she wants to continue seeing each other once we get back, but what if time apart, back in our own lives, makes her rethink that decision?

Christina grasps my hand from the passenger seat. "You know, this is the first time I feel a little sad leaving the cabin."

I press a kiss to her knuckles. "And why is that?"

She shrugs, gazing out at the snowy road ahead of us. "I was always chomping at the bit to get out of there. But being there with you, and talking with my mom ... things feel different."

Different is an understatement.

Three nights ago, I walked into a dive bar in Manhattan, bitter and jaded.

Angry at the world.

Alone.

Lonely.

Hurting.

Now, I'm heading back to the city filled with hope, a beautiful woman on my arm, and the possibility of reconnecting with my best friend.

"I feel the same way, rainbow girl."

The roads are plowed, and the ride is quick—even when I take the longest route possible.

When I pull into the spot next to Christina's snowed-in Beetle, she sits up in her seat, and twists to face me. "Let's pick a time to meet at the bar tonight. This one."

I lift a brow. "I'd like to pick you up to take you out on a date. And this isn't exactly the nicest first-date place."

She waves a hand. "Pfft. It's the place we met. It's perfect."

"And you want me to meet you here why?"

"It'll be like we're both making the choice to come here, and make this thing between us legit."

I lean over the console, and brush a strand of hair behind her ear. "You think I won't show after spending a few hours apart from you?"

Her cheeks tinge pink, and she shrugs. "I don't know."

"I like it. I'm in." I kiss the tip of her nose. "Now let's get this mini-car of yours out of the snow."

None of this makes sense.

I stare down at the disorder of words scribbled onto the paper. The other pages I'd ripped out and crumpled into balls litter the floor around me.

The words don't make sense, not yet. But I can feel it in my soul.

It came on like a tornado. Touched down out of nowhere—no warning, no signs of a storm—and I was powerless against the magnitude of its force. I was taking a shower, and the lyrics became all I could hear.

It's been a long time since creativity struck me like this. Years since I've written a song. Just as long since I've curled my fingers around the neck of my guitar, and strummed a chord.

I close my eyes, and let the lyrics come to life, swaying, pulse beating wild, as I hum the melody under my breath.

It's a sad song, but it's laced with hope.

The rainbow at the end of a devastating storm.

The light to my darkness.

The refuge for my demons.

Her. Only her.

What if she doesn't show?

I huff out a laugh, and shake my head.

Of course she'll show.

God, I hope she shows.

I glance at the alarm clock on my nightstand. The majority of my day without Christina was spent thinking about Christina. And when I wasn't thinking about her, I was creating a song about her.

I'm a fucking goner.

I throw on a pair of dark jeans, and a long-sleeve black Henley. My stomach is in knots, and it's ridiculous, because there's no reason to be nervous. I spent the past three days with this woman—seen every magnificent bare inch of her.

Yet my hands shake as I take the familiar stool at the bar.

"Whiskey neat, right?"

"Yes, please." I tip my chin. "Good memory."

The blonde bartender assesses me as she pours. "It's not every day I meet an escort in here. Kind of hard to forget."

I chuckle, and toss back the shot. "My escort days are over."

Her eyebrows hit her hairline. "How come?"

The door to the bar bursts open, and a gust of frigid air whips through the small room. A woman wrapped in a ridiculous floor-length bubble jacket stomps her boots against the wooden floor. Chunks of snow trail behind her as she makes her way to an empty stool. She's wearing a bright yellow beanie, complete with a furry pompom on top, and when she pulls it off, her dark brown hair sticks up in all directions.

"This seat taken?" she asks, dark lashes fluttering against her rosy cheeks.

"No freaking way." The bartender's eyes bounce between us. "Is she the reason you're not an escort anymore?"

"Hell, yeah, she is." My stool scrapes against the wooden floor as I stand. "You came."

That beautiful red blush flashes across Christina's skin. "So did you."

"Told you I would."

"You knew I would."

I snake my hand around her waist, settling on the small of her back, pulling her flush against me. "I missed you today."

Her cheeks burn even brighter. "I missed you too."

"So, we're doing this, me and you."

She stretches up onto her toes, and brushes her lips against mine, a feather-light touch that has my dick hardening. "We are."

I release her, and pull out the stool beside mine. She lets her jacket slide down her arms, revealing a sheer white button-up blouse speckled with holly and berries, and I can make out the red hue of her bra underneath. Every damn button is fastened, all the way up to her neck.

I'm going to rip every one of those buttons apart with my teeth.

Maybe not tonight, but *one* night.

Christina cocks an eyebrow. "You okay? You're looking a little flush."

My gaze travels down to her waist, and over her skin-tight red leather skirt. "It's suddenly very hot in here."

She giggles, and slides onto the stool. "You don't look so bad yourself, rocker boy."

The bartender leans forward, and rests her elbows onto the bar. "Well, it's nice to see you didn't get murdered."

Christina laughs. "I got lucky."

"What can I get you to drink?"

"Pinot Noir, please. And two menus. We'll be having dinner."

I thread our fingers together on the bar. "How was your day?"

"It was good. Miles made sure I filled him in on every last detail of our trip." She laughs, and her nose crinkles. "What about you?"

"Went to the gym, did some laundry, took a nap." I brush her cheek with the back of my hand. "Played the guitar for a little."

Her brown eyes widen. "You did? Oh, my God. That's great."

I smile at her excitement. "Yeah, it felt good. Strange, but good."

She tilts her head. "Do you think you'd ever get back into the music world again?"

I blow out a long, slow breath. "I've never thought about it before. I don't even know if it's in the cards for me."

"You haven't lost your talent. Lots of musicians take some time off, and make comebacks."

I smirk. "Like Justin Bieber?"

She throws her head back and laughs. "Yes, exactly like Justin Bieber." The sound of her laughter, real and honest, floats through me like the best melody I've ever heard. "And you know what? I don't think this world has seen the best of you yet. What happened to you the first time around, that was only part of your journey. You've got so much more inside you waiting to burst through."

My stomach clenches, and my chest warms. "You think so?"

She gives me an emphatic nod. "You're going to do amazing things."

No one's looked at me with this much certainty before, and with her eyes on me, there's nothing I won't do to prove her right.

Sometimes, all it takes is one person who believes in you, one person in your corner, to help you realize that all your broken pieces are worth a damn.

"I'm really happy I met you, rainbow girl."

A beautiful smile blooms on her face. "I am too."

We enjoy our meals, talking, laughing, and flirting—lots of flirt-ing—and then I walk Christina out to her car.

"I want to invite you back to my place," I say, "but I don't want to sound presumptuous."

She gazes up at me with those big brown eyes. "I was kind of hoping you'd be presumptuous."

Damn, this woman ...

"Ride with me?"

Without answering, she climbs into my passenger seat, like it's hers to claim.

It is.

We're quiet on the drive to Brooklyn, the air between us sparked with anticipation. She watches me as I drive, the weight of her stare igniting my body, and I stare at her not nearly long enough between gazing at the road. I rest my hand on her thigh, and she drags her fingers up and down my forearm. I'm thankful for the console separating us, otherwise I'm not sure we'd be able to keep our hands off each other.

Whatever happens, or doesn't happen tonight—it doesn't matter. It's not the point. I just want to hold her, to kiss her, to have her close to me. This woman makes me come alive, awakening a part of me I thought was long gone.

I toss my keys onto the entryway table when we get inside my apartment, and hang Christina's coat in the closet.

She walks in a slow circle around the living room. "You rent the entire top floor of this building?"

"I do."

"Wow. I had no idea."

I shrug, and stick my hands in my pockets. "I don't like to flaunt the fact that I have money. Makes people treat you differently."

She walks toward me, and sets her palms on my chest. "I like that you don't flaunt it."

"Come with me. I'll give you a tour later. I want to show you something."

My heart pounds harder with each step I take through the hallway, and into my bedroom. I lead her to my bed, and gesture for her to sit.

"While we were at your mom's, you asked to see a video of me playing. Figured you might want a front row seat."

She clasps her hands together as she bounces on the edge of the bed. "Yes! Will you play me the song you were working on today?"

I wink, and lower myself onto the bed beside her. "Of course."

My hands shake as I position the guitar in my lap. My fingers wrap around the neck, taking their positions on the strings, and my right hand grips the pick.

I pause, lifting my eyes to hers. "It's still in raw form."

"I understand." She places her hand on my knee. "I just want to hear you play."

I breathe in deep, letting her scent of coconuts and pineapple soothe my nerves.

And then I begin.

They told me somewhere over the rainbow,
Makes all your dreams come true.
But I didn't believe it,
Until the night that I met you.

I don't need no pot of gold,
As long as I have you to hold.
There's no battle I won't fight,
To keep your colors shining bright.
Even on my darkest day,
Nothing's gonna keep me away,
From you.
Oh, girl, from you.

I stop strumming, and my lids are slow to open. "That's all I have so far."

"Jake ..." A tear slips down Christina's cheek. "I love it. So much." She brushes her fingertips over my guitar. "You're so natural with it. The way your fingers move over the strings. It's sexy."

I grin. "Glad you think so."

She blushes my favorite color. "Do you serenade all your women like this?"

I shake my head once. "Never wrote a song about a woman before. Never brought anyone back to this apartment either."

She pulls her bottom lip between her teeth. "Why me?"

"Because no one's ever seen into my soul the way you do." I cradle her face, pressing a kiss to her forehead, to her nose, to each cheek. "No one's bothered to look. You inspire me to be better. To try harder."

At that, she stands, taking my guitar with her, and props it against the wall. When she turns back around, heat emanates from her eyes. She stands before me, twirling a strand of her hair, chewing on that luscious bottom lip.

Then she pops the top button on the collar of her shirt. "You make me feel special."

"You are."

She inches closer, and moves to the next button at her chest. "You make me feel appreciated."

"I do appreciate you."

Another button comes undone, revealing the smooth curve of her tits, creamy white against red lace. "You make me feel desired."

My breath hitches in my throat. "I do desire you."

She stands between my knees, letting another button go. "You make me feel sexy."

"*So* fucking sexy," I murmur, reaching out and undoing the next button myself.

She unzips the back of her skirt, letting it drop to the floor, while I push her shirt over her shoulders, and watch it slide down her arms.

"The world is better because you're in it, Jake Fallon."

My heart stalls, and emotion clogs my throat. No words can explain what that statement means to me.

The magnitude of it.

"You make my world better, rainbow girl. You streak through my dark clouds, and you give me hope for a better day."

She lifts the hem of my shirt, and pulls it up over my head. Her fingers blaze a trail across my skin, tracing the ink along the side of my neck, and then over the length of my collar bone, down my chest, exploring the ridges of my abdomen.

My body shudders. I cradle the back of her neck and pull her down with me as I lay back on the bed. She straddles me, caging me in with her thick thighs, and our mouths merge. Her lips are warm and soft, and I let out a groan as she rocks her hips in a slow, maddening rhythm with our kiss.

I slide my hands around her waist, and travel up her smooth back until my fingertips hit the clasp of her bra. "Can I see you, Christina?"

Her voice is breathless and desperate when she says, "Yes."

With a swift flick, the scrap of red lace falls away.

"God, you're perfect." Round, pert breasts spill over each of my palms, and I lean forward to capture a rosy nipple in my mouth.

Christina throws her head back, arching, pressing herself against me as I lick my way to give her other bud the same attention. She writhes on top of me, chasing the pleasure of the friction between us. I push aside her panties, and slide my fingers against her most sensitive spot, reveling in her wet heat. Soft, and slick, and swollen.

"Fuck, baby. You feel so good."

She grips my forearm, and rides my hand, holding me where she wants me, panting and begging for more. "Jake ..."

"I've got you." I curl a finger inside her, and lose my damn mind, rubbing and stroking, while she shoves her tits into my face.

She moans. "Jake, please. Your pants. I need them off."

We fumble to push them off together, fused at the mouth like we're trying to devour one another.

"Condom," I say. "Wallet. Back pocket."

She pulls it out, and slips it over my hardened length that's throbbing in impatient agony.

It's never been this intense before, not with anyone.

Our eyes cling for a moment, and I dive into the depths of her deep brown irises. Trust and emotion and desire churn together.

This means something.

She means something.

She climbs back on top of me, and I tease my head at her entrance, torturing myself in the process. Then slowly, achingly slow, I stroke all the way inside. She gasps, and her pussy clenches around me, squeezing me so tight.

"Fucking heaven." My head falls back against the mattress, and I grip her hips. "You feel like heaven."

She pulls back, drawing me almost completely out before she pushes herself back down, swallowing me in one swift movement. She sets the pace, showing me exactly what she likes, what she needs. Unbridled. I could watch her forever.

My hands wander over her body, caressing her face, cupping her breasts, circling her clit. I can't get enough, can't touch her enough. I want to feel everything at once. Want to feel all of her.

I sit up, and she wraps her legs around me, holding on, as I thrust in and out of her.

"I want this," I tell her. "I want you. Want to learn everything about you. Want to make you happy, give you everything you deserve. Only you, my rainbow girl. Only you."

"Yes, Jake. Oh, God. Like that."

I clutch her face, and kiss her hard, giving her all I've got until she breaks apart. She pulses around me, crying out, and clinging to me as she comes.

I give her a moment, holding her close, telling her how beautiful she is.

When she opens her eyes, a lazy smile tugs on the corner of her mouth. "That was amazing." She chews on her lip. "Can you ... will you ..."

I run my thumb along her lip, pulling it out from between her teeth. "Say it. Tell me what you want."

"Fuck me from behind, Jake."

With a hungry growl, I flip her over. She spreads her legs, pushing her plump ass in the air, taunting me. I take her waist between my hands, and plunge into her. It's bliss. Pure bliss. I thread my fingers through her silky hair, and she moans as I give it a gentle tug.

"More, Jake. Harder. More."

I pull out, and drive inside again, hard and fast. She pushes back against me, meeting me thrust for thrust. I lean forward, sliding my hands along her slick skin, squeezing her tits while I whisper filthy things in her ear. She guides my hand down between her legs, unafraid to take what she needs. I strum her like my favorite guitar, with passion and purpose, pouring all of me into her. And when I come, it's her name on my lips, the most beautiful song.

We collapse onto the bed, and she curls into my chest. Our hearts drum the same beat, our bodies and minds completely in sync.

My days have been filled with darkness. Black clouds raging overhead, winds whipping against me. I never thought the storm would pass—when you're in the eye of it, it seems like it never will. But I've learned that you can't give up. You can't stop fighting. The storm circling you will pass, as do all things in life, big and small. And when the skies clear, what a magnificent sight you'll see. Sunlight shines hope down on you, warming your face, breathing new life back into you amidst the rubble. Don't focus on the wreckage. It can all be rebuilt.

You don't want to miss out on the most incredible rainbow.

I've found mine.

My rainbow girl.

Epilogue
Two Years Later
Christina

"Are you nervous?"

Jake nods. "More nervous than usual. Making a comeback is harder than making your debut. People expect more of you."

The cheers from the crowd vibrate against the walls of the dressing room, and his wide eyes dart over to the door.

I grasp his face in my hands, forcing his emerald eyes back to mine. "Let them think what they want. You're going to blow them away."

"And how do you know that?"

"Because I know you. And I've heard your music. It's amazing."

One corner of his mouth kicks up. "That's because all the songs are about you."

I grin. "I mean, that helps."

He smooths his fingers through my hair, and cradles the back of my head. "How was your day with your mother?"

"It was great, actually. She didn't have one negative thing to say. And I know she totally wanted to comment on the smell, but I think Rachel threatened to leave her here if she upset me."

Jake laughs. "Manhattan does smell pretty bad."

"But it was nice. I enjoyed having her here. It meant a lot that she finally came to visit."

"And Miles?"

I snort-laugh. "Miles is terrified of the woman. He's convinced she put a hex on him before she left."

"She's a Catholic, not a witch."

"Eh, they're pretty much the same thing."

Jake laughs again, and I stretch up onto my toes, wrapping my arms around the back of his neck. "You're going to do amazing out there, Jake Fallon."

"I think I'm so nervous because I know my parents are out there." His Adam's apple bobs. "I just want to make them proud."

"You've already accomplished that." I press my lips against his. "And I'm proud of you too."

Over the past two years, Jake rekindled his friendship with Trent and his bandmates. It's been beautiful to watch the old friends come back together as if they didn't miss a beat. He worked hard in therapy, and made some amazing breakthroughs with his parents.

We both did. Things between my mother and I are the best they've ever been. We still don't see eye-to-eye on things—she doesn't understand why we aren't getting married and having kids, and I don't understand why any of that matters if I'm happy—but we're both trying, and that's what counts.

Jake tilts his head. "I wonder what happened to Dominick that first night we met."

"I wonder what he looked like."

"Hey." He jabs me in my side, and I squeal. "Maybe you missed out on a great catch."

I shake my head. "No. I didn't."

He dips his head, and presses a hot, sexy kiss to my lips. With his mouth on mine, he walks me backward until my shoulder blades hit the wall. He lifts me up in an effortless swoop, and I wrap my legs around his waist.

"I can't wait to get you home later," he murmurs, nibbling on my bottom lip.

Home.

Miles once thought I was crazy for feeling so strongly for someone I'd just met. But sometimes in life, the best things don't need to make sense. They just need to feel right. Love isn't logical. Your heart knows when it finds its counterpart.

The craziest decision I've ever made—hiring a male escort to bring to Christmas dinner—turned out to be the best decision I've ever made.

The door cracks, and Trent sticks his head through the opening. "Come on, you lovebirds. We're about to go on."

With a groan, Jake sets me back on my feet.

"Go show the world how incredible you are." I place one more lingering kiss on his lips, and then I make my way down to my seat.

Miles and Rachel smile when I lower myself between them.

Miles grips my forearm. "These seats are incredible. I love that you're *with the band* so we can sit in the front row."

"Best seats in the house." I smile glancing at the white tape on the stage in the shape of an X. Jake wanted me right in front of where he stands.

So I can serenade you all night, he said.

"How is he?" Rachel asks.

"Nervous. But he's going to be okay."

The lights go out, and my stomach bottoms out. The crowd goes wild, and we jump to our feet as the band strides onto the stage.

With his guitar slung around his neck, and his tattoos and ripped jeans, Jake looks every part the rock star. His messy hair falls into his eyes, and he roughs a nervous hand through it, keeping his gaze down on his guitar.

Come on, baby. You got this.

Trent's voice crackles through the speakers. "We're home, New

York!"

The noise level is deafening. Men are howling, women are screaming. The air is charged with electricity. It's a sold-out concert, and everyone's here for one main reason.

"Tonight is a very special night," Trent continues. "You all remember my best friend, Jake Fallon, don't you?"

The room erupts.

Jake lifts his dazzling green eyes, and smiles. My heart skips a beat as butterflies swarm in my chest.

His deep, raspy voice floats through the microphone. "It feels good to be back. I can't thank you all enough for your support." Then he strums the first few familiar chords, and a smile splits my face.

"This song is for my rainbow girl. I love you."

The End

National Suicide Prevention Lifeline
1-800-273-8255

* * *

Looking for something with more emotion & angst?
Keep reading for a sneak peek of my Amazon Top 30 Bestseller
What's Left of Me

New to me?
I always recommend starting with **Collision**
Book 1 in **The Collision Series**

Need something funny and light?
Check out my Amazon Top 30 Best Seller **Hating the Boss**

Want to gain access to FREE books, exclusive news, & giveaways?
Sign up for my monthly newsletter!

Come stalk me:
Facebook
Instagram
Twitter
GoodReads

Want to be part of my KREW?
Join Kristen's Reading Emotional Warriors
A group where we can discuss my books, books you're reading, &
where friends will remind you what a badass warrior you are.

Love bookish shirts, mugs, & accessories?
Shop my **book merch shop**!

* * *

All titles by Kristen are FREE on KU

The Collision Series Box Set
Collision (Book 1)
Avoidance (Book 2)
The Other Brother (Book3 – standalone)
Fighting the Odds (Book 4 – standalone)
Hating the Boss – RomCom standalone
Back to You – RomCom standalone
Inevitable – Contemporary standalone
What's Left of Me – Contemporary standalone

* * *

Chapter 1

I'm not getting out of bed today.

This is an amazing mattress. Just the right amount of firm-to-soft ratio. This comforter rocks too. It's puffy but not suffocating. These sheets are a high thread count. Breathable. I did good when I picked these out. I could stay here all day. Don't need to go grocery shopping. Who needs to eat when you have a mattress like this? Laundry? Pffft. I won't need clothes if I stay in bed. This is the perfect solution to all of life's problems.

But what is that awful smell?

A long, wet tongue slides across my cheek, and I groan. "Go back to sleep, Maverick."

With my eyelids still closed, I reach out and smooth my fingers through my retriever's fluffy fur. His tongue makes another pass over my cheek, and again, I'm hit with a blast of that stench.

My nose scrunches as my head jerks up off the pillow. "Maverick, did you eat your poop again?"

His head dips down, and he rests it on top of his front paws.

"Don't give me those eyes! They're not going to work on me this time."

He leaps off the bed and bounds into the hallway, tail swatting from left to right as he waits for me at the top of the stairs.

Guess I'm getting out of bed.

I flip the comforter off my body, swing my legs to the side of the mattress, and jam my feet into my plush white slippers.

Once I'm vertical, my head throbs like someone dropped an anvil on it. I grip onto the cool iron bannister and take my time down the spiral staircase. Maverick waits at the bottom, his body thrashing like a shark from the momentum of his tail.

"You are way too awake for me right now, bud."

He *woofs* in response and prances into the kitchen ahead of me.

When I stagger into the kitchen, sunlight streams through the windows, reflecting off the marble countertop and searing my retinas. I yank the cord on the blinds and bury my face in the crook of my elbow, hissing like Dracula.

Maverick plops down at my feet, nuzzling my ankle with his wet nose. We both jump when we hear the creak of the front door, and then he takes off into the foyer.

Paul strides into the kitchen, saturated in sweat from his morning run, and I hold my breath until his lips curve up into a smile.

"Good morning, gorgeous."

Relief washes over me. "Morning. How was your run?"

Paul snatches a water bottle from the refrigerator and twists off the cap. "Four miles today."

His royal-blue Under Armour T-shirt clings to his broad chest, the muscles in his biceps flexing with his movements. His blond strands are damp and disheveled, and his skin glows with a golden sheen.

I lift an eyebrow. "How is it that you look this sexy after a four-mile run?"

He grins. "How is it that you look this sexy when you just woke up?"

I huff out a sardonic laugh, knowing damn well I resemble the Crypt Keeper at the moment.

2

Paul leans in with puckered lips, but I make an X with my forearms in front of my face. "The poop-eating bandit got me. You might want to stay back."

He looks down at Maverick, and as if he knows we're talking about him, Maverick ducks around the corner of the island.

"You're nasty, dog."

"I'll call the vet today. Maybe they'll know how to deter him from eating his own feces."

Paul leans his hip against the counter. "I think all dogs eat their own crap."

"We have to watch him better when he's out back. Stop it before he can get to it." I walk around the island so I can start on breakfast. "I read something once that said dogs eat their poop when they're lacking vitamins in their diet. Was it an article? Maybe Josie told me. I don't know; I can't remember. Either way—"

I stop moving and snap my fingers in front of Paul's face. "Are you even listening to me?"

Paul shakes his head, his eyes roving over my body. "I haven't heard one word since you stood up in those silky shorts."

I smile and set a frying pan on top of the stove. "Please. This isn't anything you haven't seen before."

"Yet it never gets old." He closes the distance between us and stands behind me, trailing his hands up my arms.

I hum at his light touch, welcoming it. "Let's hope you always think that."

"I know I will." He tilts my head to the side and presses his lips to my neck. One of his hands slips under my camisole, cupping my breast, while he tugs my shorts down with the other.

My head falls back against his shoulder, and a long exhale leaves my parted lips. "Don't you have a meeting?"

"Just means we'll have to be quick." His fingers slide between my thighs and press inside me while his thumb rubs circles on my clit at the same time.

My legs quiver, and I reach forward to grip the edge of the counter. Paul gives my back a gentle push until my chest is pressed against the cool marble, and then he slides his length inside me.

"I love you," he whispers at my ear, gripping my hips, pumping in and out of me in long, controlled strokes.

I arch my back to meet each of his thrusts, and his fingers return to my clit as he drives into me faster, harder, deeper. I moan, writhing against his hand, and his pace quickens.

I can feel the pleasure mounting in my core, the steady build like a rising wave. Soon, it crashes over me. I cry out as the spasms rack through my body. Paul goes under too, grunting as his hot liquid fills me.

He holds me there, pressing soft kisses to my shoulder, my neck, my temple. "This is what I've missed. I'm so glad we can finally get back to how things used to be."

"Me too."

And that's my halfhearted truth.

I should relish in this feeling, the closeness, his gentle love, but my mind crawls toward the analytical place it always goes to, calculating the date, the time, the exact location in my cycle. My fingers itch to reach for my phone and click on the fertility app out of habit, but for the first time in three years, I don't.

And after last night, I never will again.

With a pat on my backside, Paul pulls away and tucks himself back into his running shorts. "I'm hitting the shower."

My eyes linger on his wide back and confident swagger as he leaves the room with his head held high, free from the anxious thoughts that plague me.

Guilt squeezes my chest when I think about everything that I've put him through over the past few years. The stress, the doctor's appointments, all my tears.

No more.

Paul's right. We need to get back to the way we used to be. Back before I became obsessed with starting a family. Before I plunged into depression and dragged him down with me. Before the people we were when we got married turned into strangers.

It's time to put it to rest.

And it's up to me to do it.

I can be better.

I can find happiness again.

I straighten my camisole, pull up my shorts, and start gathering the ingredients I need for breakfast.

The kitchen is my favorite room in this entire house. Beautiful marble countertops; tall, white cabinets; stainless steel appliances. Paul had the contractor create it based off of my exact vision. He says it's because he loves me so much. I say it's because he needs me to cook for him because Paul could burn water.

Sometimes it feels like I'm living someone else's life, like this is all a dream. Living in a mansion in Orange County, California, married to the Adonis that is my husband, not having to get up and work 9-5 every day. I'm very fortunate to have everything I could ever need at my fingertips.

I didn't grow up with all this. I came from an average, middle-class family. But when I met Paul in college, everything changed. We've been together for nine years now, and I'm still not used to this lifestyle. I don't think I ever will be.

As I scoop the egg-white-and-spinach omelet with hash browns into the glass container, Paul struts back into the kitchen, dressed to perfection in his navy suit. I hand him his lunch bag, his breakfast, and his coffee mug.

He presses his lips to the top of my head. "Thanks, gorgeous. I'll see you tonight."

"Have a good day."

"Be good, poop breath," he calls over his shoulder.

Maverick barely lifts his head from where he's sprawled out by the back door, bathing in the sunspot.

The dog-life of Riley.

When I hear the click of the front door, a long exhale whooshes out of me. I want to walk upstairs and climb right back into bed, but if I'm going to make things better, I have to start by looking the part. So instead, I drag myself up the stairs and into the bathroom.

It's been a while since I've cared about my appearance. Been a while since I've cared about anything other than becoming a mother.

Fake it 'til you make it, they say.

Flipping on the lights, I shimmy out of my pajama shorts and tear the camisole over my head. I suck in a sharp breath when my eyes land on my reflection in the mirror for the first time this morning. My stomach clenches at the sight of the dark-purple splotches along my left bicep, memories of last night flooding my vision.

Damn you, Maverick. I wanted to stay in bed today.

I blink away the hot tears before they get the chance to brim over, quick to replace the weak emotion with logic.

Paul drank too much last night, and everything we've been holding in for the last three years came to a head.

It was my fault.

I shouldn't have let things get to that point.

I shouldn't have spoken up.

I'll do better.

It won't happen again.

Needing a plan rather than wallowing in self-pity, I examine the span of the bruising and mentally scour through my wardrobe for the right sweater. Hopefully, today will be brisk enough to wear one without drawing attention to myself. Even if the weather's hot, I could get away with wearing one of my cardigans with three-quarter-length sleeves. Shouldn't be too conspicuous.

Deep breath in through the nose, and out through the mouth.

Maverick.

California king bed.

Walk-in closet.

Dream kitchen.

Yard with a pool.

Mercedes.

"I'm fine," I tell my reflection. "Everything's fine."

I twist the lever in the shower and step under the waterfall, letting the warm water cascade over my skin. By the time I lather and rinse, the urge to cry is gone and I can breathe easy again.

Wrapping the towel around myself, I swing open the bathroom

door and head to my closet. My pale-yellow sweater covers the mess on my arm, and I leave it unbuttoned over my white-and-yellow floral maxi dress. I spend thirty minutes lining my eyelids, curling my lashes, and passing the flatiron over my blond waves, taming it the way I know Paul prefers it.

With my armor in place, I square my shoulders in the mirror and heave a sigh. "Good as new."

At the sound of my sandals clunking down the stairs, my overeager dog gallops toward the front door.

"Ready for your walk, Mav?"

He *woofs* and spins in a circle.

I'm clipping his leash onto his collar when a loud *boom* echoes outside. My shoulders jolt, and Maverick jumps to scratch at the door, barking like a madman.

"Are we starting with the fireworks already?"

The Fourth of July isn't for another week. Plus, it's nine o'clock in the morning.

I push the sheer cream curtain aside and peer out the window. A white pickup truck rolls to a stop in front of Josie's house across the street. Well, there are visible areas of white paint—the truck was white at *one* time—surrounded by burnt-orange rust spots eating away at the metal. The bed of the truck is covered by a blue tarp, securing the contents underneath with a yellow bungee cord. Thick, black smoke billows from the exhaust pipe, trailing all the way down the block.

The truck pops again as it idles, sending Maverick into another barking fit.

"All right, bud. Enough." I reach down to pat his head, keeping my nose glued to the windowpane.

The driver's door swings open, and a man steps out. A navy-blue baseball cap sits on his head, pulled down low over his eyes. His plain white T-shirt, which looks more like an undershirt, is wrinkled and smudged with brown stains. His jeans are ripped—not the kind of rips people pay for—and equally as filthy as his shirt. He strides around the front bumper and up the walkway that leads to Josie's backyard.

"He must be the new landscaper."

Maverick cocks his head to the side as if he's listening to me.

Josie's Lexus isn't in her driveway, so I find it strange that she'd give a stranger the passcode to get in through her back gate. Maybe she left it unlocked for him before she left. Seems odd, but we've been desperate to find a new landscaping company after one of the workers from our old company got caught having an affair with Mrs. Nelson down the street. If Josie found someone dependable, I'm going to need his card. Paul will be thrilled. Our shrubs need trimming, and weeds are beginning to poke up through the pavers in our driveway.

"Come on, bud." I snatch my sunglasses off the entryway table and lead Maverick out the front door.

Once we cross the wide street, Maverick pulls ahead of me, his nose to the ground, sniffing his way up the path of pavers. The iron gate is ajar, and Maverick continues pulling me through the opening into the backyard.

The layout is like mine. Same-sized rectangular inground pool, similar patio furniture. But Josie's yard is full of life, whereas mine has barely been touched. Squirt guns, skateboard ramps, and balls from every sport litter her grass. It's obvious that a family lives here.

Josie often complains of the mess, but I'd give anything to step on a Lego block belonging to *my* child.

The landscaper is standing in front of the pool house with his back to me, one hand on his hip while the other tips the neck of a brown glass bottle into his mouth.

So much for finding a reliable landscaper.

I stop a few feet behind him, wrapping Maverick's leash around my hand a few times to keep him from pulling me any further.

"Don't think you should be drinking on the job, sir."

The man spins around and blasts me with a scowl that sends a shiver down my spine. Under the brim of his hat, I spot a deep, disgruntled crease that lies between his dark brows. His prominent, unshaven jaw pops, clenching, as if he's gritting through physical pain while he glares at me with piercing steel-blue eyes.

The hairs on my arms lift in a whoosh of awareness, and fear slices into me.

I shouldn't have come back here alone.

Maverick's tail thumps against my leg as he leans forward to get

8

to the stranger, clearly unfazed by the potential danger I've put us in.

"I ... I'm sorry." I pull Maverick back. "I didn't mean to startle you. I live across the street."

Great idea. Tell the nice murderer where you live.

He doesn't respond. Doesn't introduce himself. He just keeps hitting me with that unwavering glacial stare. It's too much, too powerful to withstand, so I lower my gaze and take in the rest of him.

Strong shoulders span wide, adding to his towering height. His shirt is taut around his upper-body. The muscles in his arms are well-defined striations, more than just swollen biceps and triceps. He's carved from stone, detailed and unforgiving. A work of art that people travel from all over to stand in front of in admiration.

This man is beautiful.

Then again, that's probably what every woman said about Ted Bundy right before he killed them.

I should leave. Flee back to the safety of my home.

But I'm frozen, sucked in by the enigmatic energy surging around him like a tornado of rage and agony.

And I'm standing right in his path.

I swallow, my throat thick with apprehension. "I, uh, we're in need of a new landscaper. I saw you come back here and figured I'd come ask for your card." I swallow again, my gaze flicking to the beer bottle glinting in the sunlight. "It's a little early to be drinking, don't you think? I mean, you shouldn't be impaired while operating heavy machinery. Don't want to lose a foot in the lawn mower."

I choke out a laugh, desperate to make light of the situation, but it comes out strangled and strained.

The man doesn't laugh with me. He doesn't crack a smile. Not sure his facial muscles would know how if he tried to. One massive hand is curled at his side, as if he's gripping the leash on his composure, his self-control ready to snap.

"You've got some nerve coming back here like this." The man's voice is gruff with a sharp edge, like he gargles with a throatful of razors every morning.

My eyebrows lift in a flash of irritation. "Me? I'm a potential customer. One who wants to pay you for your landscaping services. Or I did, before I caught you getting drunk on the job."

Why am I arguing with the scary man?

He folds his arms over his chest, accentuating the corded muscles in his forearms. "And you assume I'm a landscaper because why?"

"Your truck, for one." I wave my arm in front of him. "You're too dirty to be pool maintenance. If you were a roofer, you'd have a ladder." I shrug like it's simple addition. "And this isn't your backyard, so unless you're here to rob the place ..." My fingers touch my lips. "Oh, God. You're not here to rob them, are you?"

He edges closer, the look of disgust twisting his features—the look he's directing at *me*.

I lift my chin and try not to flinch.

I've learned that flinching only makes it worse.

Maverick strains against his leash, his eager nose in the air, wide eyes begging the stranger to pet him. I have to use both hands to tug him back.

Some guard dog you are, Mav! This man is about to kill me, and you're trying to sniff his crotch and make friends.

The man points his index finger at me, revulsion rolling off his tongue with each syllable. "You self-righteous, pretentious little princess."

My mouth falls open, and my stomach bottoms out.

"You stand there in your designer clothes, your shoes that cost more than a month's rent, scrutinizing everyone behind your ridiculous fucking sunglasses, and you're gonna judge *me*?" He shakes his head. "My clothes are dirty because I work my ass off. My truck's a piece of shit because I have more important things to pay for. And I'm a grown-ass man, so I'll drink whenever the fuck I feel like drinking. All you rich motherfuckers act like you're better than people like me, but I know the sickening truth. I can lay my head down at night with a clear conscience because I'm not living a lie. I'd rather look ugly on the outside than be ugly on the inside like you."

His words pack a physical punch, hitting way too close to home. A tremor rips through me, and before I can stop it, a tear escapes from under my sunglasses.

It's time to go.

"I'm sorry." I whip around and bolt out of the backyard, dragging Maverick behind me.

My legs carry me across the grass as fast as my wedges will allow. I bunch my dress in my fist, hiking it up over my knees so my strides are longer.

When I reach my house, I slam the door closed behind me and press my back against it. My chest heaves as I gasp for air, my heart racing. A sob gurgles in my throat, but I swallow it down.

Maverick.

California king bed.

Walk-in closet.

Dream kitchen.

Yard with a pool.

Mercedes.

Maverick whimpers, nudging me with his cold nose. I sink down to the floor and fling my arms around him, burying my face in the comfort of his soft fur.

"It's okay, Mav. I'm okay."

Everything's okay.

I shouldn't have confronted him like that.

It's my fault for making him so angry.

My speeding pulse returns to normal after a few minutes of deep breathing, and I push off the floor. Maverick follows me into the kitchen as I swipe my purse and my car keys off the counter.

"Sorry, bud. You gotta stay here. I'm running to the store. Making a special dinner for your dad tonight."

I kiss the top of his head, and then I'm back out the door, head down, without so much as a glance at the pickup truck out front.

11

"**M**mm. So good, babe."

My lips spread into a smile. "Figured I'd surprise you with your favorite dish tonight."

Paul's hand slides across the cherry wood table, and he entwines our fingers. "I love it. Thank you."

"How was your day?"

He tugs on his tie, loosening it, before popping his collar and slipping the loop over his head. "Good. Meeting went well. I think Haarburger's going to sign with us."

"That's great."

He dabs the corner of his mouth with his napkin. "How was therapy?"

"It went well."

His Adam's apple bobs up and down. "Did you, uh, tell her what we talked about last night?"

"I told her about our decision to stop trying to have kids. She thinks it's good that we're on the same page, that we're able to move on together."

"Not what I was referring to, Cal."

"Oh."

He's asking if I told her about the bruises he left on my arm.

I look down at my spaghetti. "No, I didn't mention it."

"Good." He sets his fork down beside his plate. "Because I meant what I said last night. It won't happen again."

I nod, unsure of what he wants me to say to that. It wasn't the first time he put his hands on me, nor was it the first time he promised that it won't happen again. I want to call him out on that. I want to ask him why he feels the need to hurt me in order to get his point across. I want to ask him why he can't control his temper. I want to ask him what happened to the sweet man I met in college. I want to ask him to get some help.

But sometimes, silence is easier than navigating around all the egg shells lying at my feet.

He picks his fork back up. "Did you call the vet?"

"I did. They said to watch him when he's in the backyard so he doesn't get the opportunity to eat his poop." I lift my goblet to my lips and take a long sip.

"Did you ask why he's doing this?"

My stomach coils. "The, uh, the doctor said it could be due to anxiety."

"Anxiety. Like you."

"Yeah. He asked if we've been stressed, because dogs can pick up on our feelings."

Recognition flashes across Paul's face, his light-brown eyes hardening. "So what did you tell him?"

"I told him everything's fine, of course. He said we could put Maverick on a low dose of anxiety medication, but I said that won't be necessary. We'll just watch him better when he's outside. Won't happen again if we keep an eye on him." I force a smile and clasp my hands together. "Ready for dessert?"

He shakes his head and pushes his chair back as he stands. "I'm going to change. Got some e-mails to send out."

"Of course. I'll get this all cleaned up."

He's gone before the sentence leaves my lips.

Could've gone worse, I suppose.

I release a sigh and begin stacking our plates.

While I rinse off the dishes in the sink, I gaze out the window into the darkened yard. The pool house at the far end elicits the memory of the bizarre encounter in Josie's backyard this morning.

I've tried not to think about the rude stranger all day, but my mind keeps drifting back to him. Back to what he'd said.

He was right. I'd judged him by his appearance and made an assumption based on it. Shouldn't have been that big of a deal, though. He could've laughed it off like a silly misunderstanding. He didn't need to go off on me like he did. People judge books by their covers all the time.

Hell, he did the same thing with me, didn't he? He lumped me in with the wealthy people in this neighborhood, pointing out my expensive clothes and accessories, calling me a fake without knowing anything about me. I could call him a jerk and chalk it up to him being mean.

But his words carry weight.

I *am* a fake.

I *am* living a lie.

Who was that man, and how did he read me so easily?

More importantly, does Josie know that someone was in her yard today?

I dry my hands on a dishtowel and dig through my purse to find my phone. Before I can tap out a text, I spot one already waiting in my inbox. When I click on it and read the words that pop up on the screen, my hand clamps over my mouth.

Josie: So I heard you met my brother this morning.

Keep reading **HERE** for more of *What's Left of Me*

Made in the USA
Middletown, DE
06 November 2022

14283933R00076